I0600463

All Through the Night

by Shirley Lauro

A SAMUEL FRENCH ACTING EDITION

SAMUEL FRENCH

FOUNDED 1830

NEW YORK HOLLYWOOD LONDON TORONTO

SAMUELFRENCH.COM

Copyright © 2001, 2010 by Shirley Lauro

ALL RIGHTS RESERVED

Cover image courtesy of the author.

CAUTION: Professionals and amateurs are hereby warned that *ALL THROUGH THE NIGHT* is subject to a Licensing Fee. It is fully protected under the copyright laws of the United States of America, the British Commonwealth, including Canada, and all other countries of the Copyright Union. All rights, including professional, amateur, motion picture, recitation, lecturing, public reading, radio broadcasting, television and the rights of translation into foreign languages are strictly reserved. In its present form the play is dedicated to the reading public only.

The amateur live stage performance rights to *ALL THROUGH THE NIGHT* are controlled exclusively by Samuel French, Inc., and licensing arrangements and performance licenses must be secured well in advance of presentation. PLEASE NOTE that amateur Licensing Fees are set upon application in accordance with your producing circumstances. When applying for a licensing quotation and a performance license please give us the number of performances intended, dates of production, your seating capacity and admission fee. Licensing Fees are payable one week before the opening performance of the play to Samuel French, Inc., at 45 W. 25th Street, New York, NY 10010.

Licensing Fee of the required amount must be paid whether the play is presented for charity or gain and whether or not admission is charged.

Stock licensing fees quoted upon application to Samuel French, Inc.

For all other rights than those stipulated above, apply to: Abrams Artists Agency, 275 Seventh Avenue, 26th Floor, New York, NY 10001, Att: Peter Hagan.

Particular emphasis is laid on the question of amateur or professional readings, permission and terms for which must be secured in writing from Samuel French, Inc.

Copying from this book in whole or in part is strictly forbidden by law, and the right of performance is not transferable.

Whenever the play is produced the following notice must appear on all programs, printing and advertising for the play: "Produced by special arrangement with Samuel French, Inc."

Due authorship credit must be given on all programs, printing and advertising for the play.

ISBN 978-0-573-69802-6   Printed in U.S.A.   #29308

No one shall commit or authorize any act or omission by which the copyright of, or the right to copyright, this play may be impaired.

No one shall make any changes in this play for the purpose of production.

Publication of this play does not imply availability for performance. Both amateurs and professionals considering a production are strongly advised in their own interests to apply to Samuel French, Inc., for written permission before starting rehearsals, advertising, or booking a theatre.

No part of this book may be reproduced, stored in a retrieval system, or transmitted in any form, by any means, now known or yet to be invented, including mechanical, electronic, photocopying, recording, videotaping, or otherwise, without the prior written permission of the publisher.

MUSIC USE NOTE

Licensees are solely responsible for obtaining formal written permission from copyright owners to use copyrighted music in the performance of this play and are strongly cautioned to do so. If no such permission is obtained by the licensee, then the licensee must use only original music that the licensee owns and controls. Licensees are solely responsible and liable for all music clearances and shall indemnify the copyright owners of the play and their licensing agent, Samuel French, Inc., against any costs, expenses, losses and liabilities arising from the use of music by licensees.

Music and lyrics for "All Through the Night" and "Es zittern die morschen Knochen" are in the Public Domain.

IMPORTANT BILLING AND CREDIT
REQUIREMENTS

All producers of *ALL THROUGH THE NIGHT must* give credit to the Author of the Play in all programs distributed in connection with performances of the Play, and in all instances in which the title of the Play appears for the purposes of advertising, publicizing or otherwise exploiting the Play and/or a production. The name of the Author *must* appear on a separate line on which no other name appears, immediately following the title and *must* appear in size of type not less than fifty percent of the size of the title type.

ALL THROUGH THE NIGHT premiered in New York City on October 2, 2009 at the Marjorie S. Dean Little Theatre. It was produced by the Red Fern Theatre Company, (Melanie Moyer Williams, executive artistic director). The production was directed by Melanie Moyer Williams, with sets by Adrienne Kapalko, costumes by Emily DeAngelis, music arrangement by Kristin Lee Rosenfeld, and lighting design by Jessica Greenberg. The cast was as follows:

GRETCHEN. . . . . Theo Allyn

ANGELIKA. . . . . Hana Kalinski

FRIEDERIKE . . . . Michelle Lookadoo

LUDMILLA . . . . Lesley McBurny

FRAU LEHRERIN/FRAU DIREKTORIN/
    FRAU FUHRERIN/FRAU OBERAUFSEHERIN. . . . . Andrea Sooch

CHARACTERS

LUDMILLA – She moves in and out of play from age nineteen to adulthood, but since she is the storyteller, she is somewhat ageless, moving through time and in and out of all time frames as she tells her tale. A heartland, rural woman. Fair, plump, good-natured. Funny, likeable, down to earth peasant, great Mother Wit. Has an intimate relationship both with audience and characters. Slight German accent; speaks English as a modern Mrs. Malaprop.

GRETCHEN – From 14-16 to adulthood. Fair. Very poor, clever, ambitious. Grows tough as steel. Desperate needs to be counted, important, recognized, drive her to do anything to better herself. Becomes a 200% Patriot. But loses her soul. No accent.

ANGELIKA – 14-16 to adulthood as a nurse. Fair. Naïve, innocent adolescent who sees life with cup half-full. Giggly, happy, grows to be religious, ethical adult. Fragile mentally and shaken in faith briefly but gains strength to feel God is with her as she goes against the regime. No accent.

FRIEDERIKE – 17-18 to adulthood. Fair. An aristocratic background. High-spirited teen-ager; spunky, slightly haughty with dare-devilish quality. As she matures. she leaves her aristocratic class and heritage, dissenting to take high risks against the regime. A survivor. No accent.

NOTE: It is suggested the above actresses be cast somewhere in their midtwenties in order to stretch back and forth in time. They are somewhat aged at beginning and end of play, but should rely on inner feelings of age, rather than any attempts to physically age or use of make-up, etc. to denote age.

THE FOLLOWING CHARACTERS ARE PORTRAYED BY ONE ACTRESS:

FRAU LEHRERIN – Headmistress/Teacher. Old maid. Nervous. Eccentric, but under control, in command of herself. She has embraced Fascism all the way. It has given her great opportunity to become a Head Mistress in The New Order. She now has power. When this is threatened, she becomes enraged and outraged, but usually keeps this contained. She maintains strict discipline, the mode of education of The New Order. She now can mold her student's destinies, as she sees fit. German accent.

FRAU DIREKTORIN – Director at clinic for mentally/physically handicapped German children. Her father founded the clinic, and she inherited it. As new regime takes hold, Nazis take over the clinic, but she's allowed to stay – at least for the present – if she adheres to the new medical and scientific philosophy of the Reich. She is making great effort to accept their New Direction of Science and

Medicine, carrying out all orders of Nazis at the clinic. But slightly conflicted with moral and ethical problems as she does this. Gentle, somewhat sympathetic in manner – to a point. German accent.

FRAU FUHRERIN – High ranking administrator for Frauenwerk – the National Party Organization to train and support the country's women in carrying out the ideology of The New Order, in their homes, churches, schools, hospitals. One of select group of women in party. Has power psychologically, ideologically to carry out harsh punitive actions against any women resisters. Haughty, vain, demanding. A sexual aura to her. She is consciously aware she can manipulate her position to satisfy her own needs of power, control, sexuality. Government's given her license to let these needs be satisfied and she does. Attractive, sexually alluring. German accent.

FRAU OBERAUFSEHERIN – Head Concentration Camp Guard. Overwhelming lust for power and control, accommodated by the Regime's legitimization of all sadistic impulses. She is sanctioned and rewarded by her government for acting out on any prisoner, her unbridled, full-blown savageness, by torture and/or annihilation of her helpless victims. A cruel tyrant. Sophisticated in her cruelty. Knows exactly what she's doing. German accent.

NOTE: The age of the actress playing these roles can be anywhere from forties to late fifties. Must have energy, power, vigor. In no way a "Grandma" type.

All the characters' stories are true although all the characters are fictional. Their stories have been inspired by actual interviews and oral histories.

SETTING

The idea of a Wagnerian type mountain as a metaphor, may be a good departure point for this surrealistic type play. Or a city in ruins. Some sort of surrealistic abstraction in which perhaps lights which could give us illusion of someone in the dark and shadowy crevices of caves of a mountain or rubble – emerging into brightness as they come into focus in the story. And/or use of depth and coming forward into light to suggest coming down a mountain to enter a scene. Various levels, with platforms, some high; and ramps, steps could be helpful.

All characters always somewhere onstage. Can be in shadows, behind rubble, pieces of scenery, under ramps, platforms – seen in silhouette, nearly obscured when not in scene. Ludmilla sits closest to audience at kitchen table on raised platform on one side of stage. But moves, closer to action of individual scenes, or stands obscured, then moving closer, sitting or standing near where a scene may occur. Enters the scenes of the past at designated times. Important she not be in one stationary spot throughout. She doesn't overhear scenes. Presence at all times of all characters suggests the communal experience they have shared. They should appear, be half seen or be obscured in terms of focus of each scene.

FURNITURE: Minimal. Possible use of two or three stools, chairs, tables, benches –maybe less. Could be done with almost no furniture, using ramps, platforms of set to sit on. Same furniture used in different scenes. Ludmilla's stool and kitchen table, however, shouldn't move, unless she moves it, and should be used by no other characters.

TIME AND PLACE

Before the times and places of war, during war and afterward.

AUTHOR'S NOTES

Play is not realistic or conventional.

Surrealistic in style.

The structure of the piece rests on the government's ever encroaching negative force and power within the story, on the minds, hearts and finally lives of the other characters.

I would like to dedicate this play to
"The survivors who lived to tale this tale."

"The murderers are loose! They search the world. All through the night, oh God! All through the night!"

– Gertrud Kolmar. Perished in Auschweitz.

ACT I

(LUDMILLA enters in bright lights. She wears large bakery apron, headscarf, could carry signs in a basket.)

LUDMILLA. *Guten Tag!* Hello!

(She looks at sign, pleased, sits on stool by small kitchen table, smiles at audience, delighted to have listeners:)

So? Tonight I tell you *mein* story: "Happily Ever After!" *Und* maybe you wanna listen? I betcha, I betcha!

(She hangs up a sign somewhere that says:)

*(***"ONCE UPON A TIME"***)*

(Smiles at audience, sits, takes bowl, from kitchen table, stirs, looks back to audience again. Smiling:)

So? You listening?

(looks around audience)

Gut! Gut! Well, then – Once upon a time, a long, long time ago, there lived, on top of the mountain there –

(She looks up.)

A mean old man. *Und* nobody knew exactly how he got up there so quick *und* so high. All we knew was one day we was looking up – *und* there he was! *Und* there was his league in addition! *Und* he was looking down on *us* – watching *every thing* we was doing. *Und* then? He started in *mit* his rules. *Und* we couldn't do this *und* we couldn't do that – *und* we had to do this *und* we had to do that! Until pretty soon we couldn't do any things hardly what *we* wanted! *Und* his gang? They was total in control making them rules *happen! Und* everybody was scared. How we live "Happily Ever After" now? We was asking. *Und* in addition? He hated so many peoples – he made the rule some peoples didn't get to live no more at all! *Ja.* Well.

(She stirs an ingredient into bowl.)

LUDMILLA. *(cont.)* So this is a long time ago – *und* now is different! Now? I think we is getting to live "happily ever after," I betcha! I betcha!

(She chuckles.)

Und tonight? In *mein* story? We gonna find out *for sure* if now the peoples –

*(She now sees, coming from shadowy area, **FRAU ANGE-LIKA**, nurse's white apron, scarf of African fabric, large cross around neck. Carries black nurses bag, stethoscope around neck. She's walking along a road. **LUDMILLA**, excited, calls to her:)*

Hey, hey Angelika!

(to audience)

Oh, you gonna like Angelika!

ANGELIKA. *(recognizing her)* Frau Ludmilla? *Guten Tag!*

LUDMILLA. You could help me tell *mein* story, "Happily Ever After?" On account, you're happy over there in Africa, *ja?*

*(**ANGELIKA** stops, looking at her.)*

ANGELIKA. I make a small contribution here in Africa, Ludmilla. It's gratifying to me. Carl and I and our family have lived here for ages. We have a clinic: "Soweto Obstetrics"! I just came from a home delivery. And we have women lining the clinic waiting room every day for care.

LUDMILLA. So you perfect for *mein* story: "Happily Ever After" – remembering first on things to tell about then –

ANGELIKA. When?

LUDMILLA. When – "Once upon a time, a long, long time ago, on top of the mountain,

(She glances up.)

Was this old guy *und* his league!"

*(She looks at **ANGELIKA**.)*

LUDMILLA. You remember *him, Ja?*

ANGELIKA. Who?

LUDMILLA. Hey – you're supposed to tell about him *und* his league – when he is living on that mountain – this is how *mein* story starts –

(Beat. **ANGELIKA** *shrugs:)*

ANGELIKA. I don't know who you mean – I don't know what to say –

(Moves away as suddenly a bluish, unreal light in another area, higher, something resembling balcony with arch that opens. **FRAU LEHRERIN** *suddenly appears:)*

FRAU LEHRERIN. Fräulein Angelika! Answer! *Antworten Sie mir!*

(Hears from on high, behind her. Not looking back at her.)

ANGELIKA. *(to self)* Frau Lehrerin – my old teacher – ?

(She begins slowing back up toward **LEHRERIN**.*)*

LUDMILLA. *(to audience) Ach!* She was head of the school… *und* she was in league *mit* him…

FRAU LEHRERIN. You have been assigned to recite our new confession and new pledge, Fräulein – for the parade –

(Still not looking up back slowing backing up towards **LEHRERIN***:)*

ANGELIKA. School parade – ? But that's a lifetime ago – the week she took Frau Friedmann's job –

FRAU LEHRERIN. Today our *first Bund deutscher Mädel's* parade takes place, Fräulein.

(continuing to back toward **LEHRERIN**, *growing more and more fearful:)*

ANGELIKA. The German Girls Club?

FRAU LEHRERIN. A unique privilege: Our new leader – the Führer – comes to *our* ceremonies! *We* will see him in person! And *you* have the honor of reading our new confession and our new pledge in his very presence! You have practiced these at home, *ja?*

(shaken, frightened, begins to sink into the past, looking at her)

ANGELIKA. *Ja, ja,* Frau Lehrerin –

FRAU LEHRERIN. So, we will rehearse. Put on your school apron and your new Girl's Club jacket. *Schnell.*

(**ANGELIKA** *slowly reverses apron to school apron. Puts on militaristic Girl's Club jacket.*)

ANGELIKA. *Ja – ja* – Frau Lehrerin —

FRAU LEHRERIN. Look at me.

(**FRAU**'s *eyes grip* **ANGELIKA**. *She's sinking to the past.*)

The jacket is not buttoned correctly.

(**ANGELIKA** *fiddles with buttons, looking at* **FRAU**.)

FRAU LEHRERIN. *Kommen Sie hier!*

(**ANGELIKA** *into bluish light of the past: a schoolgirl.* **FRAU** *buttons her jacket. Then lights on scene up, normal as* **LUDMILLA** *hangs sign:*)

("SCHOOL DAYS")

FRAU LEHRERIN. Now this afternoon we march to the Village Square in file. There you wait until your name is called. You then come on the platform, curtsy before the Führer, walk to the podium – and begin our ceremony with the new recitation I gave you. "Our Confession." Then follow with "Our Pledge." Start!

ANGELIKA. *(reading, without understanding or agreeing with what she reads:)* "Our Confession." We b-b-believe only in N-N-National So-so-socialism." "National Socialism is the great – faith of our nation. The – the Führer is our – our – Savior? He – he will save and protect us forever. National Socialism is – is taller than any ch-ch-church – ??

(She's findng words absurd, hard to believe, starts stumbing on them.)

More *ancient* than any – ch-ch-church – ??

FRAU LEHRERIN. You are hesitating? Stumbling?

ANGELIKA. It's – it's hard Frau Lehrerin – new ideas all of a sudden – they make no sense – "taller than –

FRAU LEHRERIN. You will never question our confession, Fräulein! It is unpatriotic! Disrespectful! This is no longer Frau Friedmann's class where traitorous, degenerate, liberal views were discussed. This is now the school of the government. You understand?

ANGELIKA. *Ja, ja,* Frau Lehrerin...

FRAU LEHRERIN. So. Study this in your free periods this morning, until you are perfect, and respectful of what you say. So. Now our pledge, which you will recite second on the platform.

ANGELIKA. *(She's sliding out of control it's so funny.)* "We will be German – We – w-w-will be – puh-puh-pure – We will be faithless – faithful!!"

(She can't go on, bursts into giggles.)

FRAU LEHRERIN. You now are giggling?

ANGELIKA. I – I can't help –

FRAU LEHRERIN. You will now add three punishment marks to your punishment book for this stumbling and giggling and disrespect! This makes you subject to a punishment for your disloyal, unpatriotic attitude. What this will be I will determine tomorrow. Sit!

(ANGELIKA sits.)

And now at the ceremony – Fräulein Gretchen will receive a music medal if she sings our new song perfectly. You are prepared to rehearse now, Gretchen?

(Light on FRAU GRETCHEN sitting somewhere, half in shadow, dressed in gray cloak, blending into shadows although we see her face in profile, drinking liquor from a bottle.)

LUDMILLA. *(looking to GRETCHEN)* Hey – Gretchen? Gretchen? You won that music medal when the new teacher came to the school!

(GRETCHEN doesn't answer, drinks more.)

So – you could be in *mein* "Happily Ever After" story, I betcha!

(GRETCHEN drinks more then looks at her.)

GRETCHEN. I don't know what you're talking about. I live in the house where I was born. I take care of old women who pay to live there. I cook for them, wash for them, iron, scrub the floors. I sleep on a cot in the hall

(She turns profile again, sips liquor again.)

LUDMILLA. You got to remember that medal on account once upon a time you sang at the parade when you first saw the Führer *und* won it! *You* used to wear it sometimes points in fact.

*(**GRETCHEN** looks at her, coughs.)*

GRETCHEN. *That* medal? My *grossmutter's.* An heirloom.

(She turns, starts drinking.)

FRAU LEHRERIN. *(in bluish light, smiling)* Fräulein Gretchen?

GRETCHEN. *(turning slowly, recognizes voice, dreads sight)* Frau – Lehrerin??

FRAU. *Achtung!*

*(**GRETCHEN** turns away.)*

ACHTUNG! You hear me?

GRETCHEN. *(slowly rising) Ja* – Frau Lehrerin – *ja, ja* –

FRAU. Your uniform?

*(**GRETCHEN** doffs coat, girl's club uniform beneath.)*

Your scarf – *and* hair?

*(**GRETCHEN** undoes pug, braid falls down, her eyes gripped by **FRAU**'s. She's in the past: the school girl. Enters blue light near **FRAU**, then lights up, normal.)*

FRAU. *Kommen Sie hier, Fräulein!*

*(**GRETCHEN** to her)*

FRAU LEHRERIN. So. Fräulein, the music medal will be presented to you on the platform…if you have learned the song perfectly. So – rehearse now as you will sing it.

(GRETCHEN turns to ANGELIKA, then looking out starts singing Nazi Youth song. She starts softly, hesitantly, gains strength, superiority as she sings:)

GRETCHEN.

Es zittern die morschen Knochen

Der Welt von dem roten Krieg.

Wir haben den Schrecken gebrochen,

Fuer uns war's ein grosser Sieg!

Wir werden weiter marchieren,

Wen alles in Scherben faellt,

Denn heute da hoert uns Deutschland,

Und morgen die ganze Welt!

FRAU LEHRERIN. *Sehr gut!* And now the recitation of the song?

GRETCHEN. *(quality of superiority now, can recite or sing)*

While the rest of the world still trembles,

From the blood and rot of War,

We have crushed *our* weakness to pieces!

And now? *Our* Victories will soar!

We will become fiery Conquerors!

And the Reich in Triumph will *shine!*

So *sing* all the people of Deutschland:

"Tomorrow the world is mine!"

FRAU LEHRERIN. *Sehr gut!* You have learned it perfectly. The music medal will be yours! *Bund deutsche Mädel* – our German Girls Club meeting now ends and we have a short school recess.

(She's moved into a shadowy area near her office. GRETCHEN modeling uniform. To ANGELIKA:)

GRETCHEN. I'm getting the medal, Angelika!

(ANGELIKA turns to her.)

ANGELIKA. *Wunderbar,* Gretchen!

GRETCHEN. And – at the Girl's Club *I'm* dressed just like the *Mayor's* daughter. So now? *I'm* just as good as she is. And so are you!

ANGELIKA. *(happy, laughing)* We are! We are!

GRETCHEN. But *I'll* be even better because *I'll* be wearing the medal. Come on – we'll practice how we'll march at the parade! You know the new step?

> **(GRETCHEN** *singing, marching Nazi goose step,* **ANGELIKA** *joins* **GRETCHEN**, *giggling.)*

GRETCHEN. *(cont.)* See – it's not what our lives are today, Angelika, it's how we will live them *tomorrow* that counts! That's what our new government and our Führer are bringing us – a future!

ANGELIKA. He got in by just one vote though – some people even say he stole the election.

GRETCHEN. Don't ever repeat that! That's not patriotic! He got voted in to fix our country!

> *(close to* **ANGELIKA**, *whispering:)*

My veteran hero Papa? The Führer is going to help him!

ANGELIKA. Yes?

GRETCHEN. Papa lays in bed – no legs – no control –

> *(She's getting outraged:)*

NO ARMY PENSION OR MEDICAL CARE from that war! It's me and my brother must *bathe* Papa, *diaper* him, *change his sheets* three times a day! And my poor mother? She scrubs *Banker Isaac Moses* mansion to support us! *He* 's not patriotic! *He's* not a real German. He's a Jew that got RICH off that War! But now? Our family will get its pension. And Papa? Medical care!

> *(She laughs.)*

And me? *I* can be BIG! IMPORTANT IN THIS WORLD! AND MAKE MY PAPA PROUD!

FRAU LEHRERIN. Fräulein Gretchen? *Kommen Sie hier!*

> *(ANGELIKA turns away, to shadows. GRETCHEN eagerly up to FRAU who opens a small box dangling the medal.)*

GRETCHEN. *Ja*, Frau Lehrerin?

FRAU LEHRERIN. In addition to winning the medal, I'm giving you also a perfect grade in music, Fräulein, which puts you first in your class – and permits me, if I choose – to submit your name for the class of "Higher Expectations" next year… You have great ambition for this class, *nicht?*

GRETCHEN. *Ja, ja,* Frau Lehrerin.

FRAU LEHRERIN. So? What is this "Higher Expectation" you have?

GRETCHEN. *(shy to admit this dream:)* Maybe a teacher too… like you…history…biology too…like you…

FRAU LEHRERIN. Teacher? Veterinarian is the "Higher Expectation" for which *I* aimed as a girl. *Ach* – such an *instinct* I had to find sickness in the animals – do away with them before they infected the others! But a *girl…* no encouragement…poor family – I could barely work my way through to be a teacher –

GRETCHEN. I see –

FRAU LEHRERIN. *(She breaks memory, turns to* **GRETCHEN***.)* But now? *I* am headmistress! And – we will see where *your* "Higher Expectations" will take *you, Ja?*

(She grows confidential.)

You understand – The Party is now taking over *every* girl's organization *all over Germany. Bund deutsche Mädel* will soon be everywhere. *Und* after graduation – I am now in a position to recommend you for a Party *job* with the new Girls Clubs, Fräulein. Good salary. A place from which you could climb.

GRETCHEN. *(ecstatic, controlling it) Vielen Dank!* Frau Lehrerin!

FRAU LEHRERIN. You might even transfer to Berlin –

*(***GRETCHEN*** starts imagining this, trying to contain her extreme joy.)*

Many new opportunities are now opening up there – if you continue to prove yourself!

GRETCHEN. *Ach!* I will, Frau Lehrerin!

(FRAU looks at GRETCHEN, retreats in archway, subtly beckoning her closer. GRETCHEN comes.)

FRAU LEHRERIN. *(a confidential whisper now:)* Our government now has power to let me promote a loyal girl like you!

(She studies her:)

You family is loyal, too?

GRETCHEN. *Ja, ja.* Party members, Frau Lehrerin. *Our* family records are perfect; we are all members of the party, we go to all meetings, obey all the new laws!

FRAU LEHRERIN. Because we can now open mail, tap phones, check medical records, civil records, churches, societies people belong – to find suspected dissidents, traitors to the Reich...

GRETCHEN. You can check our family records everywhere if you want!

(a beat)

FRAU LEHRERIN. So I can count on you to help me serve the Reich – as the Reich will serve you?

GRETCHEN. *Ja, ja,* Frau Lehrerin!

FRAU LEHRERIN. *(coming closer, whispering)* Any girls you see – or suspect of degeneracy or dissent: actions – words – deviousness? Report them to me for investigation at once?

(GRETCHEN nods, runs to shadowy area. FRAU LEHRERIN takes jewelry box, moves toward LUDMILLA.)

Und Frau Ludmilla?

LUDMILLA. *Ja, ja?*

FRAU LEHRERIN. You received a medal then, too –

LUDMILLA. *Nein* – not me.

(She looks at FRAU LEHRERIN, slightly fearful, confused.)

FRAU LEHRERIN. However – an honor for your *Mutter, Frau Dietrich* – nearly the same thing.

LUDMILLA. What – ?

FRAU LEHRERIN. When you were a girl – you came here to receive your *Mutter*'s honor – The *Mutter's* Gold Cross –

(FRAU now dangles large gold cross on chain, LUD-MILLA gasps at sight, not taking eyes from cross.)

LUDMILLA. *(shaken, mesmerized by swaying cross, remembering)* The Gold Cross – the *Mutter's* Gold Cross – The Gold Cross –

FRAU LEHRERIN. So – you do recall –

(Beckoning LUDMILLA into past, swinging cross as lights shift bluish on FRAU LEHRERIN as LUDMILLA slowly rises, eyes never leaving swaying cross.)

FRAU LEHRERIN. So? Put on your Girls Club uniform, Fräulein. *Und kommen Sie hier!*

(LUDMILLA slowly reverses bakery apron, and scarf to bright side. She's the young FRÄULEIN LUDMILLA. She puts basket with cake on handlebars of bike, parks it near FRAU, comes into blue light too.)

But you do not put on your uniform, Fräulein.

FRÄULEIN LUDMILLA. I don't got one, Frau Lehrerin.

FRAU LEHRERIN. But you are a *Bunde Deutsche Mädel, nicht?*

FRÄULEIN LUDMILLA. *Nein!* A simple country girl. I don't even finish school – I got to help out home – the bakery –

FRAU LEHRERIN. So. A good German daughter!

FRÄULEIN LUDMILLA. *Vielen Dank* Frau Lehrerin.

(Lights up to normal.)

FRAU LEHRERIN. *Und* what great pride you must take in your *Mutter!*

FRÄULEIN LUDMILLA. *Ja*, well, she made ten *Kinder* for the Reich!

FRAU LEHRERIN. Exactly what the Führer wants: as many *kinder* for a powerful Germany as every woman can produce.

FRÄULEIN LUDMILLA But she can't have no *more* the doctor says. We hardly got no room for what we got. Me, Willi, Hilde, Heinz – *und* then the *first* twins – which *I* am naming: *Herta – und – Berta!*

(She laughs, proud at her invention. **FRAU** *manages a forced smile, wants to leave.)*

Und see? For the twins? *DIE MUTTER'S* BRONZE CROSS! Then Ernst, Rudolph *und* comes *DIE MUT-TER'S* SILVER CROSS! *Und* now? *More* twins *I* am naming: *HANNALORE und ANNALORE! Und Mutti* gets *DIE MUTTER'S* GOLD CROSS!

FRAU LEHRERIN. So. You and your *Mutter* will come to the platform at the parade to receive the cross.

(Silence. **FRAU LEHRERIN** *looks around.)*

FRAU LEHRERIN. Your *Mutter* is not yet here?

FRÄULEIN LUDMILLA. *Nein.*

FRAU LEHRERIN. She is at home with her twins?

FRÄULEIN LUDMILLA. She is in bed *mit* her stroke.

FRAU LEHRERIN. Stroke?

FRÄULEIN LUDMILLA. Two weeks yesterday when the twins is coming *und* Dr. Ginsberg is so kind and staying all night? Face to foot left side *Mutti? Kaputt!* But some-day, Dr. Ginsberg is promising, he's gonna help her move again! *Und* I betcha, I betcha he's so smart he's gonna make it happen! "Only she's 42," he says. "*Und* too fat *mit* diabetes, in addition."

FRAU LEHRERIN. So. Well. *You* will come and take the honor for her at the parade, *nicht?*

FRÄULEIN LUDMILLA. *Nein.* I got to go work at the bakery. See, *Mutti* never was thinking she's getting so many *Mutter*'s crosses and so many *Kinder!*

FRAU LEHRERIN. *(wanting to leave:)* Oh…?

FRÄULEIN LUDMILLA. *Ja, ja!* When she is getting married – before these laws on having babies? She is planning two – three *kinder* tops. On account she was wanting to run the bakery! She bakes good *Kuchen und Brot und* likes talking *mit* the Village womens who comes in – *aber* now she's in bed *und* can't talk hardly no more at all.

(She looks around.)

Aber – I can't stay here no more. *I* got to go run the whole bakery. *Ach!* I forgot something.

(goes to bike, takes basket with cloth over it)

Best cake Dietrich's got! Nuts, raisins, ginger spice – a piece for every girl!

(FRAU LEHRERIN *puts cross in box, hands her box.)*

FRAU LEHRERIN. Congratulations!

FRÄULEIN LUDMILLA. Ja, *vielen Dank* –

> **(FRÄULEIN LUDMILLA** *leaves. Bluish light then normal lights as she sits,* **LUDMILLA,** *the woman.* **FRAU LEH-RERIN** *to shadows as lights on* **FRIEDERIKE,** *outside, wearing bright sweater. Turns on old portable pho-nograph softly, starts writing on pad. Music: "Ain't Misbehavin'".* * **FRIEDERIKE** *sings.)*

LUDMILLA. *(to her)* Hey – Frau Friederike?

(to audience)

She's "The big time journalist"! Berlin. The most best newspaper!

(to her)

Und you living fancy, I betcha, I betcha? Perfect for *mein* story: You is *famous!*

FRIEDERIKE. *(laughing lightly)* My husband and I live in Berlin, Ludmilla. He's an art dealer. My daughter, Franziska, plays the violin in the Philhar-monic…a pretty apartment – some fascinating friends – an interesting life –

(She smiles turns up phonograph a bit lights cigarette, starts writing again.)

Somehow this music gets me in the mood to write –

LUDMILLA. That's from when you was a girl

(to audience)

Count *und* Countess von Strohmer was her parents. *Und* they was living in such a big castle in our little vil-lage nobody could hardly believe somebody's in there,

* See Music Use Note on Page 3.

LUDMILLA. *(cont.)* excepting maybe Kings *und* Queens! *Und* when our bad times comes in Germany, the Count brings Friederike home from Swiss Boarding School to be safe in our Village school –

FRIEDERIKE. I hated that village school! They said, it was good once. But when I came? The Nazi government had just taken hold of it. The party line was being stuffed down our throats 'til we choked! And we were punished if we blinked an eye! *I'd* been taught so differently in Switzerland – free, able to express my thoughts – ideas –

*(**FRIEDERIKE** turns from these thoughts, picks up pen, writing pad, turns phono up, writing, singing to music.)*

*(**GRETCHEN**, the schoolgirl, suddenly pops up from behind something. She's in blue shadows of the past:)*

GRETCHEN. *(tauntingly)* Jazz? From *Untermenschen* American negroes?

FRIEDERIKE. *(stunned)* WHAT?

GRETCHEN. Like Jesse Owens!

FRIEDERIKE. *(completely bewildered)* I beg your pardon?

GRETCHEN. And at school!

FRIEDERIKE. School?

(Looks around, slight wary now. Puts out cigarette.)

GRETCHEN. And such a *jazzy* sweater you're wearing too!

*(**FRIEDERIKE** removes sweater.)*

FRIEDERIKE. WHO ARE YOU?

*(**GRETCHEN** comes closer, taunting:)*

GRETCHEN. I'm Gretchen!

*(She catches her eye. **FRIEDERIKE** staring at her now, shaken somehow.)*

FRIEDERIKE. Gretchen – but – you – you're so far in my past – Gretchen – ?

GRETCHEN. You better put that phonograph away! It's *verboten!* Someone could report you.

FRIEDERIKE. Report me?

GRETCHEN. *(taunting her more)* Yes!

FRIEDERIKE. To who?

GRETCHEN. Frau Lehrerin.

*(**FRIEDERIKE** begins slowly, warily to rise; remembering – starts sinking into past.)*

FRIEDERIKE. Frau Lehrerin? She's from the past, too –

(Sinking more into past, growing more wary, she stands.)

GRETCHEN. *(cocky)* If they hear the music? Anyone could report you to her any minute!

*(**FRIEDERIKE** frightened now, puts on school scarf.)*

FRIEDERIKE. But – they won't –

GRETCHEN. Why not?

*(**FRIEDERIKE** laughs as adult, but then laughs again, eerily – her school girl laugh. She now joins **GRETCHEN** in the past bluish light, then lights up, normal. She's the young **FRIEDERIKE**.)*

FRIEDERIKE. Because – because of who we von Strohmers are and how we are connected. And where.

*(**GRETCHEN** looks at her a moment, then goes to phonograph.)*

GRETCHEN. Where'd you get the phonograph anyhow? And where's that record from? And what's it doing here besides?

FRIEDERIKE. *(wary)* Why?

GRETCHEN. Only teasing!

(She laughs, runs to where phonograph is.)

Must be fun to own all this though, huh? See, you're not the only one here that likes swell American music…

FRIEDERIKE. "Swell"? American slang now? From such a little Nazi?

(She sings, does a little goosestep, imitating **GRETCHEN**'s *song:)*

"*Und Morgen die ganze Welt!*"

GRETCHEN. My *parents* are the Nazis!

FRIEDERIKE. Mine have joined the party, too. Donating money to Hitler. And – all of a sudden they're selling thousands of acres of our forests to the military – and getting millions back – which we don't even need! They've changed. "Patriotic," they say.

GRETCHEN. But mine *make* me belong! Don't you think I'd like a phonograph? Records? Sing American songs – like you?

FRIEDERIKE. Want me to teach you one?

*(**GRETCHEN** looks around.)*

GRETCHEN. *Ach!* Frau Lehrerin might hear – and murder me!

FRIEDERIKE. She's giving you the music metal.

GRETCHEN. But last year when *mutter's* working late – I don't do *any* homework! Then she gave me enough punishments to kill a cow!

*(**FRIEDERIKE** stands to go, pulls long strand of pearls from her pocket, puts them on, takes off school scarf.* **GRETCHEN** *looks at her, admiring the glamorous spirited* **FRIEDERIKE**:*)*

GRETCHEN. Pearls? Where're you going?

FRIEDERIKE. Berlin.

GRETCHEN. Berlin?? *Gott im Himmel!* It's lunchtime! You're supposed to go home to the Castle – bring flags for the parade – you promised to make flags for the whole class .

FRIEDERIKE. *(laughing)* Our seamstress is bringing them. I'm meeting her by the school gate before afternoon session.

GRETCHEN. But what if Frau –

FRIEDERIKE. *(cutting in)* Frau Lehrerin won't know the difference – don't worry.

(She starts away.)

GRETCHEN. Where you going in Berlin anyhow?

FRIEDERIKE. Buy more American records – listen to live jazz!

GRETCHEN. *(flabbergasted)* Where?

FRIEDERIKE. In a cellar – where they're rehearsing –

GRETCHEN. "They"?

FRIEDERIKE. The "Swing Boys." Practicing "The Harlem Sound." They play at night at "The Jazz Note" a *verboten* club now! Used to be a swanky place to go. Now – it's "*degenerate!*"

(She laughs with mischievous excitement.)

GRETCHEN. You'll be back for afternoon session?

FRIEDERIKE. Of course – I've done it before –

GRETCHEN. Then take me?

*(**FRIEDERIKE** starts away again.)*

Gott im Himmel! TAKE ME!

*(She's trailing **FRIEDERIKE**.)*

I never get to do one thing. I just work and get punished, Friederike! School – home? Please?

*(**FRIEDERIKE**, enjoying her power, feeling generous, stops:)*

FRIEDERIKE. Well then – watch your time. *Komm schon!*

*(They go to rehearsal cellar area, as in background we hear "St. Louis Blues." **FRIEDERIKE** sings, as they enter Cellar, stay at entrance peering in. **FRIEDERIKE** recognizing musicians waves, greets them, continues.)*

"St. Louis woman, with her diamond rings ..."

*(**FRIEDERIKE** moves into cellar, **GRETCHEN** at entry, looking around.)*

GRETCHEN. *(Amazed. Giggling. Whispering to **FRIEDERIKE**)* *Gott im Himmel!* Friederike? These boys have hair down to their ears!

FRIEDERIKE. Mmm –

(Dancing as she sings or hums, which continues through rest of scene.)

"She pulls my man around, by her apron strings – "

GRETCHEN. *(whispering to* **FRIEDERIKE***)* And they're smoking one cigarette after the other after the other!

(She watches, spots something:)

Look! *That* cute boy at the piano? He's smiling at me – pointing to the records –

FRIEDERIKE. Come on – follow me –

*(***GRETCHEN*** moves into cellar starts to sing with* **FRIEDERIKE***, then moves to music, but hesitantly.)*

FRIEDERIKE & GRETCHEN. "*We* got the blues, *we* got the blues, *we* got the St. Louis Blues, blue as *we* can be –"

*(***FRIEDERIKE*** is looking at someone.)*

GRETCHEN. The boy's still smiling – wants *me* to have a record – should I speak to him? Take it?

FRIEDERIKE Keep dancing, Gretchen!

(They dance, sing a little together. But **FRIEDERIKE** *now moves away, solo, singing, moving toward someone. She's connected. To* **GRETCHEN** *but watching boy:)*

FRIEDERIKE *That* one's new. They say his name is Franz. And what he's doing is 'scatting' on his bass viol!

*(***GRETCHEN*** *trailing her, trying to get her attention:)*

GRETCHEN. Friederike – maybe I could take the record – *you'd* keep it for me? Play it for me sometime at the Castle?

FRIEDERIKE. *(not really listening now)* " 'Cause the man I love, has gone so far from me – gone so far, gone so far gone so – far – "

(She is focused on the boy but speaking to **GRETCHEN***:)*

Ach Gott: he's soo handsome! Look! He is watching me move! Gazing at me! Intensely! Strumming and strumming while I am moving and moving – to his beat!

(singing to boy:)

"Got the blues yes I do, yes I do, oh you know that I do –"

GRETCHEN. *(whispering to* FRIEDERIKE:*)* That record – Friederike – would you –

FRIEDERIKE. *(oblivious, cutting* GRETCHEN *off)* Such deep blue eyes. So sympathetic! He is different! Overwhelming!

(She dances away from GRETCHEN, *toward boy.)*

"Got the blues, got the blues, got the St. Louis blues – "

*(*GRETCHEN, *feeling very rejected, trying to get her attention:)*

GRETCHEN. Please?

*(*FRIEDERIKE *totally involved now with Franz.* GRETCHEN *looking at watch.)*

Afternoon session's starting – we have to go –

FRIEDERIKE. *(brushing her off, eyes on the New Boy) Ja, ja –* see you in school – "Because the man I love – he's gone so far from me – gone so far – gone so far –

*(*GRETCHEN *moves away, stops, watching, feeling betrayed.* FRIEDERIKE *still jiving. Music stops. To self:)*

Franz – coming to me – ?

(as if speaking to him)

"Coffee at a cafe? – well – just for a little while then – a little while –

(As FRIEDERIKE *leaves,* GRETCHEN *runs to* FRAU LEHRERIN *on balcony.* GRETCHEN *whispers to her.* FRAU *nods, then rises.)*

FRAU LEHRERIN. *Achtung! Klasse* will assemble! *Achtung!*

*(*ANGELIKA *then* GRETCHEN *run to schoolroom, standing in row.* FRAU LERHRERIN *comes forward with schoolbooks.)*

FRAU LEHRERIN. *Guten Tag, Mädchen.*

ANGELIKA & GRETCHEN. *Guten Tag*, Frau Lehrerin

FRAU LEHRERIN. *Hinsetzen!*

> *(They sit.)*

FRAU LEHRERIN. We will start the Afternoon Session with our oral test.

> *(She comes closer, looks around.)*

Fräulein Friederike? Fräulein Friederike?

> *(**FRIEDERIKE**'s not there. **FRAU** makes checkmark in book.)*

So. First instead, we review our history lesson from our new text: the recent War of 1914. Fräulein Angelika reads first. Page 98. All stand!

ANGELIKA. *(standing, reading in sing-song)* "We were stabbed in the back by the French with their so-called 'Treaty of Versailles'! Behind it? The Jew traitor with his Gypsy thief slaves who now control the world."

FRAU LEHRERIN. From now on? *Always* think of this! *Always* hold this in your mind – because this is the way it was. Sit!

> *(**ANGELIKA** sits.)*

This will now be documented scientifically as we turn to true and authentic information from our new biology textbook

> *(reading:)*

"The Proofs of Racial Science": page nineteen. Here we will learn the true nature of why we have just expelled all Jewish girls from our school! All stand!

> *(The **GIRLS** stand, open new books.)*

Who reads?

> *(**GRETCHEN** raises hand.)*

Fräulein Gretchen?

GRETCHEN. *(enthusiastically)* "The repugnant features of the Jew to avoid, root in the nose, and dark, short, fat bodies, and physical, and mental, moral diseases."

FRAU LEHRERIN. And the scientific information on Gypsies?

GRETCHEN. "The Gypsy nation is a dark, parasitic, foreign body as well. They carry diseases like rats do and they are thieves such as the world has never seen. We must stay away from them and their contagious filth!"

(**FRIEDERIKE** *sneaks, sliding into school. Stands with others.*)

"They are all *Untermenschen!* Subhuman. We must protect clean Aryan blood from all contact and contamination with all Jews and Gypsies. We must be patriots and preserve our country only for –"

(**FRAU LEHRERIN** *seeing* **FRIEDERIKE**:)

FRAU LEHRERIN. Fräulein Friederike! So. The reason you are late?

(silence)

Antworten sie mir! ANSWER!

FRIEDERIKE. I – I missed the bus coming back from the castle. That bus is always late – and I –

FRAU LEHRERIN. *(interrupting) Genug!*

(scrutinizing her more)

And the flags?

FRIEDERIKE. *(looking around)* Didn't the seamstress bring them? I told her –

FRAU LEHRERIN. *Jetzt ist aber genug!* You are not going to the castle for lunch. You are going in a cellar in Berlin.

(**FRIEDERIKE** *shoots a hard look at* **GRETCHEN**.)

There you are hearing non-Aryan men play *verboten* American Negro music. There? You made a certain friendship with a Gypsy boy – going with him to a café.

FRIEDERIKE. *(stunned)* Gypsy?

(FRAU LEHRERIN looking hard at GRETCHEN.)

FRAU LEHRERIN. Mixed blood! The worst!

FRIEDERIKE. I didn't know Franz was Gypsy. I –

(She stops short realizing what she's admitted.)

FRAU LEHRERIN. So – you *were* there. And have neglected your duty to bring the flags! Now? No one has them to march for our first presentation to honor the Führer. Your grades are now lowered 20%, Fräulein –

FRIEDERIKE. I can't believe that – I won't be able to go to the University or –

FRAU LEHRERIN. *(interrupting:)* And your *Vater* will be immediately notified of your extreme, deviant behavior

FRIEDERIKE. *(terrified)* MY *VATER*?

FRAU LEHRERIN. You are so surprised, Fräulein? So. Now the New Order has come to power, and I have come to this school, you learn your first hard lesson from the Reich: "Whoever does not bend, breaks"!

FRIEDERIKE. Please, Frau Lehrerin, don't! Please? Besides afternoon session's just starting, isn't it? I don't think I delayed anything import –

FRAU LEHRERIN. *(interrupting)* What you delayed is the oral test.

(glances at watch)

The hour is late – the parade beginning shortly.

(to other girls)

Klasse is therefore excused from the test. *Und* school ends early as I promised you. You have now the special privilege of the parade – *und* the ceremonies with the Führer. *Gehen Sie!*

(They all start out. To **FRIEDERIKE***:)*

FRAU LEHRERIN. *You* will take it. *Kommen Sie hier!*

*(***FRIEDERIKE** *moves closer to* **FRAU***.)*

First question: What will come after the Third Reich?

(**FRIEDERIKE** *rattled, quickly blurting out, not thinking.*)

FRIEDERIKE. The Fourth Reich?

FRAU LEHRERIN. There is no Fourth Reich!

(*She is enraged, tries to keep control of self:*)

"THE THIRD REICH IS THE THOUSAND YEAR REICH! A NEW WORLD ORDER PARADISE THAT WILL LAST *FOREVER*!"

FRIEDERIKE. (*blurting out again, then trailing off:*) But only Gypsy women with their tea leaves know – the – future –

(*Silence.* **FRIEDERIKE** *realizes what she's said. A longer silence.* **FRAU LEHRERIN** *is smoldering but brings herself under control, between her teeth:*)

FRAU LEHRERIN. In my office! *Schnell!*

(**FRIEDERIKE** *runs through* **FRAU LEHRERIN**'s *arch.* **FRAU LEHRERIN**, *following as* **GRETCHEN** *and* **ANGELIKA** *come running into schoolyard on way to parade.*)

GRETCHEN. (*to* **ANGELIKA**) Come on!

(*She looks at her.*)

Where's your jacket?

ANGELIKA. (*lightly*) I – I leant it to someone.

GRETCHEN. Day of the parade?

ANGELIKA. But Elsa can't even go!

GRETCHEN. (*shocked*) You gave your jacket to the Jew girl? She's not even at school anymore!

ANGELIKA. We've planned it out! She'll stand in the crowd near the platform and give it back to me – before I go up to read. She's even blond. No one will know she's Jewish. No one will even notice what we're doing – not with the Führer there!

GRETCHEN. You're wrong!

ANGELIKA. She's nice. And *she* wants to go very badly. And you know she can't go anywhere anymore – school, parades, library, park, cinema –

GRETCHEN. *(can't believe this:)* You really gave your Girls Club jacket to the Jew girl?

ANGELIKA. *(unperturbed)* Don't make such a fuss. She's my good friend.

GRETCHEN. You do a stupid thing, Angelika! You should be afraid. Elsa's not one of us – only loyal to her own people! A traitor! Frau Lehrerin is the party's new Headmistress. She can do *anything* she wants to you. Get smart! Get your jacket back!

ANGELIKA. We are church goers. My whole family. God teaches me Elsa is my equal! Frau Lehrerin can't make me obey what the government says instead!

*(**FRAU LEHRERIN** appears, in hat, going to parade.)*

FRAU LEHRERIN. Why are you not at the parade?

GRETCHEN. We are just going, Frau Lehrerin. *Aber* – Angelika hasn't put on her jacket –

*(She looks at **ANGELIKA** as if to say: get jacket!)*

Yet –

*(Silence. **ANGELIKA** doesn't move.)*

FRAU LEHRERIN. Why do you not put on your jacket?

(silence)

Antworten Sie mir!

*(More silence. **ANGELIKA** frightened now, realizing implications of what she's done.)*

ANSWER!

ANGELIKA. *(whispering)* Elsa wears it…

FRAU LEHRERIN. *(astounded)* Elsa? Where? She's been expelled.

ANGELIKA. *(whispering)* By the platform –

FRAU LEHRERIN. *(confused)* *Where* ??

ANGELIKA. At the parade –

*(**ANGELIKA** looks down. **FRAU** can't believe this. **GRETCHEN** starts backing away.)*

FRAU LEHRERIN. THE PARADE?? NEAR THE FÜHRER??

(**ANGELIKA** *nods, paralyzed, looking down. Silence.*)

KOMMEN SIE HIER!

(**ANGELIKA** *goes close to her, head still down.*)

STAND STRAIGHT!

(**ANGELIKA** *does.*)

LOOK AHEAD!

(**ANGELIKA** *does. She has epaulettes and BdM emblems sewn on her shirt.* **FRAU LEHRERIN,** *enraged, rips them all off, tearing shirt badly, knocking* **ANGELIKA** *off balance so she stumbles, regaining balance as* **FRAU** *continues:*)

In that fashion this same shirt is worn until instructed otherwise!

(**ANGELIKA** *nods, stands, clutching cross. We hear band music.*)

Now you will immediately go and find this Jew girl. Get the jacket and instruct her to leave the parade area at once – Understand me?

ANGELIKA. *Ja*, Frau Lehrerin.

FRAU LEHRERIN. Then – bring the jacket back here! *Und* stand on this spot until I return from the parade! Starting tomorrow – until further notification? All privileges of the Girls' Club will be denied you: parades, prizes, summer retreats, camping, festivals, songfests! *Gehen Sie!*

(**ANGELIKA** *runs out.* **FRAU,** *recouping, to* **GRETCHEN.**)

You are able to read the pledge and the confession with no mistakes?

GRETCHEN. *Ja, ja*, Frau Lehrerin.

FRAU LEHRERIN. Then *you* will read them from the platform in place of Fräulein Angelika. Now go at once to the parade and take your place in line before it starts!

(**GRETCHEN** *goes,* **FRAU** *straightens suit, leaves as* **FRIEDERIKE** *enters disturbed.*)

FRIEDERIKE. Ludmilla? My *Vater* has had me and Franz spied on! The phone, our servants, people in Franz's building. For weeks! Since Frau Lehrerin told him about the Jazz club. And I love *Vatti*, Ludmilla! And *Mutti!* But I don't – I can't think their way –

LUDMILLA I know – I know –

FRIEDERIKE. *Tonight?* Poppi burst into my room – pulled me from bed –

(She starts reliving scene. As father, heavy German accent:)

FRIEDERIKE. *(cont.)* "You are sleeping with a Gypsy in Berlin! *Und* I have reported him for a work camp!"

(to **LUDMILLA***)*

Poppi said the Gestapo broke right into Franz's room tonight and took him away! No warrant! Nothing! Then Poppi began screaming at me:

(as if father:)

"YOU HAVE GONE AGAINST THE REICH WITH THE SCUM OF THE EARTH! Shamed the von Strohmer name to THE PARTY your mother and I have embraced! TO THE STATE WE HONOR!! YOU HAVE STAINED US DOWN THE GENERATIONS AS TRAITORS!"

(half to self, half to **LUDMILLA***:)*

I turned away from him, Ludmilla, to leave the room. He banged the door shut – grabbed me – turned me around –

(as father:)

"YOU WILL RECANT! JOIN THE PARTY! MINGLE ONLY WITH ARYAN MEN *ONLY*! UNTIL A SUITABLE HUSBAND IS FOUND!"

(as herself, half to self, half to **LUDMILLA***:)*

But I wouldn't look at him – said nothing – wouldn't agree to what he wanted. Then – then – he pushed me from him – threw open the bedroom door –

(as father:)

"The von Strohmer name is no longer yours! This home is no longer yours! The Gestapo will be called if ever you set foot near the castle gates again! *HERAUS!*"

(Turns away, reversing school apron to work apron, scarf. Starts sweeping. To **LUDMILLA** *as goes to shadows:)*

FRIEDERIKE. *(cont.)* Frau Lehrerin expelled me – I've rented a little cell like room in Berlin where the workers live...just now found a maintenance job at a clinic. Biding my time, Ludmilla – biding my time –

LUDMILLA. *(to audience, smiling broadly:)* So – Friederike is "biding her time" – when a friend of Franz sends her a letter.

*(***LUDMILLA***, smiling, puts up sign.)*

("HIGHER EXPECTATIONS")

Ja, ja!

*(***FRIEDERIKE*** *returns, pulls out letter, reading:)*

FRIEDERIKE. "Go to the Central Library."

LUDMILLA. *(to audience)* There ain't hardly no books left in the library no more. On account they is burning them up. They don't want peoples reading nothing but what the government wants. So –

FRIEDERIKE. *(reading)* "Ask assistant Rolf to recommend a Nazi book, so you don't draw attention. He will know what to do."

(She runs to shadowy area.)

LUDMILLA. *(to audience) Und* so? She is getting the book *und* looking inside. *Und* you know what?

*(***FRIEDERIKE***, excited, runs to* **LUDMILLA** *with book and note.)*

FRIEDERIKE. A note from Franz! Smuggled from the camp!

(reading note:)

"Put *Reichmarks* inside cover. Return it. Check out whatever Rolf suggests next. Put more *Reichmarks* in *that* book, return it. *May be a way!* Your, Franz"

(She runs to shadows again.)

LUDMILLA. *(to audience)* So? Now? Friederike goes to that library again – *und* again – *und* again – keeps on asking for them "Nazi books."

(She chuckles. **FRIEDERIKE** *appears with book.)*

FRIEDERIKE. I'm saving almost all my salary, Ludmilla! Putting 100 *Reichmarks* in every book I return. I'm living on nothing now – but our dream: join the Bolshevik communists and fight the Reich!

(She runs to shadowy area.)

LUDMILLA. *(to audience, chuckling) Und?* Next?

(FRIEDERIKE *runs to her, whispering:)*

FRIEDERIKE. Franz's on a new Camp detail in the forest near a road. And THE GUARD CAN BE BRIBED! For 200 *Reichmarks* a prisoner walked right out of the forest last week.

(FRIEDERIKE *gets bike, walks it, stop. Looks in distance. To* **LUDMILLA,** *still whispering:)*

Him! Head shaved, so thin, stupid prison uniform! But HIM!

(She looks around, then very confidentially to **LUD-MILLA.***)*

We make love in the grass. He holds me so close I can't breathe.

(looks to him, waving, as he leaves:)

Aufwiedersehen – 'til next week? I love you, Franz –

(blows him a kiss, goes to shadows)

LUDMILLA. *(to audience) Und* they meets again the next week *und* the next *und* the next!

FRIEDERIKE. *(returning excited, whispering:)* We've almost enough money! *We*'re going to go Uboat – Underground to Holland!

(She starts running, calling back:)

Soon – soon – soon –

(As **ANGELIKA,** *happy, bursts in. School scarf, apron reversed to nurse's apron, scarf.)*

ANGELIKA. Ludmilla? I'm a *nurse!* Like my *mutter!* A *Catholic hospital!* And I'm in love! And getting married!

LUDMILLA. *Sehr gut!*

ANGELIKA. A fine man – Dr. Carl Schenk! And – Catholic – like me! I'm very religious now, Ludmilla. More than before – from helping the sick. And Carl's religious too.

(ecstatic)

We have a dream: "AFRICA! To help the worst suffering people of this world!"

(Happy, She runs to shadows, disappears.)

LUDMILLA. *(to audience, winking, very happy:)* A Mutual Admiration Society happening here? I betcha, I betcha! *Aber* – such a short mutual! Two months and her Carl goes to the Army. Then? Another mutual:

(She puts up sign.)

("THE STORY OF LITTLE HANS")

She is expecting!

(She laughs as **ANGELIKA,** *ecstatic, picks up baby basket, comes to* **LUDMILLA.** *)*

ANGELIKA. My beautiful baby, Hans! I brought him home early from the hospital, Ludmilla. They wanted to keep him longer but I'm a nurse. I can take better care of him myself. Somehow – I just don't trust that hospital as much –

(talks to Little Hans in basket as puts basket down with Teddy Bear in it)

See what *Mutti* got you? A Teddy Bear! *Ja, ja!* My wonderful baby, Hans! *Mutti* will take the best care of you in the world!

LUDMILLA. *(to audience) Und* she does! Best care! Best care! *Und* so – time is going by –

*(***ANGELIKA** *steps away, looking in distance.)*

ANGELIKA. Ludmilla? I am noticing something now. He is starting to walk –

(She looks in distance again, watching Hans as does **LUDMILLA.** *)*

LUDMILLA. *Ja?*

ANGELIKA. His foot turns in. I just took him to the doctor in fact. He says not to worry. He'll outgrow it.

LUDMILLA. *Sehr gut!*

(to audience)

Und she has a *sehr gut* Doctor, too.

ANGELIKA. A minor birth injury to his hip they are telling me. But, if I want to be certain – "Take him to be examined at Schlierheim," the doctor says. "The University Clinic at Heidelberg!"

(She starts to clinic area with Teddy Bear. She's excited, happy, calling back:)

They're the best, Ludmilla...then I won't worry anymore.

*(***ANGELIKA** *arrives at clinic, sits.* **FRAU LEHRERIN** *morphs to* **FRAU DIREKTORIN,** *changing in view, to clinic coat, followed by* **GRETCHEN** *in shorter clinic jacket, carrying clipboard, x-rays.* **DIREKTORIN** *in glasses, a bit flustered, shuffling papers, they go to* **ANGELIKA.** *)*

FRAU DIREKTORIN. *(smiling, always a gentle voice)* Willkommen! Willkommen! Frau –

(She puts her glasses on, glancing at document **GRETCHEN** *gives her.)*

Frau Angelika!

*(***ANGELIKA** *nods. They shake hands.)*

So, sit? Please? Be comfortable?

*(***ANGELIKA** *does.* **FRAU** *indicates* **GRETCHEN.** *)*

I am Frau Direkotrin. I have been here many years – but my assistant is new –

GRETCHEN. *Willkommen!*

> (**FRAU** *glances short-sightedly at a clipboard* **GRETCHEN** *gives her.*)

FRAU DIREKTORIN. Now then – ah – I see both you and your husband trained at the Hospital of St. Martin's?

ANGELIKA. *(proud and happy) Ja, ja.*

FRAU DIREKTORIN. Among the foremost! I knew several staff members that trained there. Dr. Braunmann – Dr. Mueller? But they – they are not there now – I don't think…

ANGELIKA. St. Martin's *was* a wonderful place to train. *Wunderbar!*

> (*She bursts out laughing.*)

My husband and I? We met there.

FRAU DIREKTORIN. *Ja?* And your boy was born there?

> (*looks again at record*)

No – I see Kronheim Maternity – also top of the list!

ANGELIKA. *(smiling, proud) Ja,* it was!

> (*beat*)

FRAU DIREKTORIN. Well…look – about Hans – the doctors have done an X-ray –

> (**GRETCHEN** *hands it to her; She holds it up, hesitantly pointing things out:*)

– And – unfortunately – they have found *here*? A permanent damage in the left hip joint: the cause of the limp –

ANGELIKA. So, maybe a little correction can be done? Special shoes? A brace? When they're ready, we'll come back.

> (*She rises.*)

FRAU DIREKTORIN. *(This is hard for her:)* Well – they have said – the damage is permanent …

ANGELIKA. But it's just a little limp. Millions of people have little limps!

FRAU DIREKTORIN. I'm so sorry, Frau Angelika – But I'm afraid the orthopedic and internist's report says the hip is destined to degenerate –

(buries head in report, affected by this, reading:)

"Probable prognosis: limp becoming more severe – crutches – wheelchair – bedridden…"

ANGELIKA. It's a mistake!

FRAU DIREKTORIN. They do say *"probable."* But – for now –

(She reads again:)

"A permanently handicapped child" – with "slurred speech and hearing loss" noted by our best Psychiatrist in Psychological Tests – together with a "Confirmation of child retardation."

ANGELIKA. Not Hans! He's extremely smart! He speaks very quickly, he is so smart. Maybe this is what they *mistake* for "slurred" and "retardation"!

FRAU DIREKTORIN. A hard dose to swallow – but we all must trust our new psychiatrist – and all the latest theories –

*(**ANGELIKA** rises, clutching Teddy Bear.)*

ANGELIKA. I will take Hans to another clinic. A second opinion!

(She starts heading toward a door to Interior of clinic.)

FRAU DIREKTORIN. This distinguished clinic is the one to which you were referred, Frau Angelika…and Hans' papers are officially filed here…it will make trouble…

*(**ANGELIKA** stops. Then:)*

ANGELIKA. We'll file in Berlin! The best doctors of all are in Berlin!

(She hurriedly starts looking now for the area Hans might be in.)

FRAU DIREKTORIN. But don't you see – it official. Stamped on his official birth record!

*(**ANGELIKA** stops.)*

Our doctors have *all* reached the same conclusion: admittance as an inmate of this –

ANGELIKA. INMATE??

FRAU DIREKTORIN. Resident, then? Look, they have instituted visitation every Sunday...stay all day...bring a picnic – play in the garden.

*(**ANGELIKA** now is running from one level to the next, frantic:)*

ANGELIKA. HANS? HANS?

FRAU DIREKTORIN. Everyone is specially trained here – the very latest techniques and equipment to work with children like Hans.

*(**ANGELIKA** stops, facing her.)*

ANGELIKA. *Where is my son?*

*(**DIREKTORIN** confidentially now, softer:)*

FRAU DIREKTORIN. I beg you? Don't resist. Then there may well develop a question of your legitimacy as a parent. Don't you see?

*(**ANGELIKA** sees ward entrance, starts toward it.)*

ANGELIKA. No, I don't see.

(She keeps going toward ward.)

Hansy?? HANSY!!

FRAU DIREKTORIN. Don't risk this!

(beat)

Please? Should you question the diagnosis here – you will be deemed unpatriotic! Flirting with treason!

*(**ANGELIKA** stops.)*

ANGELIKA. TREASON?

FRAU DIREKTORIN. *(whispering)* You are aware German citizens have limited choices. Allegiance to the flag, the Führer, the Reich. To choose anything else is to be a traitor. Guilty of treason.

ANGELIKA. I am a loyal German. My family's been here hundreds of years! My *Vater* died in the first war. My husband's already a doctor with the Wehrmacht! It's insane to think I could be a *traitor!*

(FRAU shuffles through papers.)

FRAU DIREKTORIN. But both your husband's and your medical backgrounds could be easily turned against you.

ANGELIKA. WHAT?

FRAU DIREKTORIN. The State may well ask how you two of all people could deny your child medical treatment at birth? And now deny him care *here* – the foremost clinic of its kind in the Third Reich.

ANGELIKA. My medical background is why I want another clinic's opinion! Where is he?

(She goes to another entryway to interior of clinic.)

HANS??

FRAU DIREKTORIN. Take him away and you are even giving them grounds for taking away *your* nursing credentials!

ANGELIKA. WHAT?

FRAU DIREKTORIN. And grounds for "extreme neglect." A child abuse case.

ANGELIKA. ABUSE?

FRAU DIREKTORIN. The regime may choose, to assign more loyal guardians.

ANGELIKA. What are you telling me?

FRAU DIREKTORIN. That they may decide to give the child to what the Reich determines is a wholesome German upbringing – while they incarcerate you as an enemy of the state.

ANGELIKA. What's going on here all of a sudden? I was a nurse in hospitals. I know what it should be like here! And my husband and I? We have rights! We are his PARENTS!

(A silence. FRAU looking at her, then kindly, softly:)

FRAU DIREKTORIN. I am seeing this happen to many parents besides you now –

(Beat. **ANGELIKA,** *looking at her, near tears.* **FRAU** *puts arm around her shoulder, sits her back down.)*

ANGELIKA. I – I only want what is best for him – don't you see that?

*(***DIREKTORIN*** *nods to* **GRETCHEN** *who gives* **ANGELIKA** *form and pen. Takes Teddy Bear.)*

DIREKTORIN. And "what is best" is often so painful to do, *nicht?* For all of us –

(She turns away affected, then turns back:)

Sign? I am able to offer him admittance at once if you do. And we'll speak again Sunday ? A few days only. I promise, Frau Angelika, I personally will do my utmost for Hans – and you –

(Silence. **ANGELIKA** *looks from* **DIREKTORIN** *to* **GRETCHEN** *to form. Reluctantly signs, hands form back.* **DIREKTORIN** *raises arm quietly, in salute, then* **GRETCHEN.***)*

DIREKTORIN. *(softly:) Heil Hitler!*

GRETCHEN. *Heil Hitler!*

(Reluctantly **ANGELIKA** *salutes.)*

ANGELIKA. *Heil Hitler!*

*(***FRAU DIREKTORIN,*** **GRETCHEN** *with Teddy exit.* **ANGELIKA** *moves away to other area.)*

LUDMILLA. *(calling to her:)* Angelika? Angelika? How was Little Hans when you visit him today?

*(***ANGELIKA** *looks at her, calling:)*

ANGELIKA. I *think* everything is going very well, Ludmilla! I stay all day Sundays – Hans seems happy – and Frau Direktorin ordered him special shoes – *Handmade* from Berlin!

*(***ANGELIKA** *goes. To audience:)*

LUDMILLA. So months is passing in this way – excepting one Sunday when she goes …

(**ANGELIKA** *returns to clinic area as* **DIREKTORIN** *comes forward with* **GRETCHEN**. **FRAU** *takes* **ANGELIKA**'*s hand.*)

FRAU DIREKTORIN. Oh – Frau Angelika – I was just looking for you – I – I am so sorry, Frau Angelika – but the doctors have had to put your son in isolation.

ANGELIKA. What?

FRAU DIREKTORIN. *(thumbing through papers)* They told me the liver is not completely systematic.

ANGELIKA. *Liver?* He's a very healthy boy!

FRAU DIREKTORIN. I thought so too – but…well…they have diagnosed him with jaundice. These things do set in suddenly. you know, with children – assistant?

(**GRETCHEN** *clears throat, reads from clipboard.*)

GRETCHEN. Dr. Reinstadt reports: Tuesday. Third March. Discoloration of pupils and skin observed. Temperature: 102°. Test 45B ordered. Liver dysfunction – possible.

FRAU DIREKTORIN. Dr. Reinstadt suspects hepatitis. Highly contagious. He's already ordered quarantine. I will immediately inform you when diagnosis is confirmed – and as soon as visitations are possible. I hope just a short while.

(**DIREKTORIN** *hurries out,* **GRETCHEN** *behind her.* **ANGELIKA** *looking one way then another as* **FRIEDERIKE** *appears, sweeping floor. They exchange smiles.* **ANGELIKA** *whispering:*)

ANGELIKA. I want to see my son – Hans Schenk? Could you help me?

(**FRIEDERIKE** *looks at her, disturbed, then looks around, nods, whispering:*)

FRIEDERIKE. They're making rounds.

(*She points direction to room, looks around.*)

If they come? You found the room yourself. *Schnell!*

(Looks both ways, hurries to hallway, keeping guard as **ANGELIKA** *finds room, kneels by Hans' crib.)*

ANGELIKA. Hansy? HANSY? *Mutti* is here to take care of you now – *Liebes Kind?*

(looks at him, gasps)

ANGELIKA. *(cont.)* Straight jacket? Face yellow!

(bends down to him)

BRUISES? *ACH GOTT!*

(Screams, pulls restraints. **FRIEDERIKE** *enters with Teddy, puts hand over* **ANGELIKA**'s *mouth.)*

FRIEDERIKE. Shh!

ANGELIKA. They've hit him!

FRIEDERIKE. *(looks around, whispering:)* That's the least of it! The SS's has taken total command now.

ANGELIKA. Frau Direktorin?

FRIEDERIKE. I don't know. But the other doctors – nurses? A new Nazi staff obeying – in secret – every time the SS winks and nods.

ANGELIKA. What do you mean?

FRIEDERIKE. The hepatitis is a sham! The Nazi doctors gave Hans three red crosses when they first examined him.

ANGELIKA. Three red crosses?

FRIEDERIKE. "Incurable." "Euthanasia" – a club foot. There's no state money to support useless life – they say. Old people, mentally disturbed, disabled –

ANGELIKA. What?

FRIEDERIKE. The only value they see in Hans? *Force poison down him* – experimental drugs for the military. To see how much the organs can take before he's dead!

ANGELIKA. *GOTT IM HIMMEL!* MY BABY?

ANGELIKA. THEY ARE SAVAGES!

FRIEDERIKE. I do what I can – help mothers get their children out –

ANGELIKA. But Germany's *his* country!

FRIEDERIKE. No more!

> *(Sound of door shutting)*

They're on the floor. Untie him.

> **(ANGELIKA** *does, grabs baby, a bundle wrapped in blankets.)*

FRIEDERIKE. *(cont.)* Side door's not locked. Go!

> **(ANGELIKA** *starts out.)*

GOTT! The other way!

> *(Sound of another door shutting close by.* **ANGELIKA** *goes other way.)*

Hide by the river. At six they're at dinner. Then run – take the first train that comes – *Schnell!*

> *(She hands her Teddy,* **ANGELIKA** *runs to shadows crouching. Then, looking at bundle that is Hans:)*

ANGELIKA. *(to self) Gott im Himmel!* He's choking blood – limp – blue – eyes rolling back – he's gone!

> *(Sobbing, she covers him, clasping Teddy. Crouches, obscured in shadows as* **DIREKTORIN** *rushes into Hans' room,* **GRETCHEN**, *behind her.)*

FRAU DIREKTORIN. Strip his bed. We must not leave a trace.

> **(GRETCHEN** *doesn't move, staring at empty bed.)*

Well, they said he was contagious!

> **(GRETCHEN** *stands head down, affected, whispering:)*

GRETCHEN. I – I did not think he was retarded when he first came. Only his foot turned in a little – He was a sweet little Hans –

FRAU DIREKTORIN. He was.

> **(GRETCHEN** *stifling tears, turning to her.)*

GRETCHEN. And I didn't think he was sick from hep –

FRAU DIREKTORIN. *(interrupting)* Hepatitis? That was the doctor's diagnosis!

> **(GRETCHEN** *can barely speak.)*

GRETCHEN. But that strange medicine – if he wasn't forced to swallow it he –

FRAU DIREKTORIN. *(interrupting)* Don't say that – don't even think that. It was the most advanced medicine in all the Reich – but the Hepatitis attacked him severely. He was destined, I was told…

(She looks at her.)

Well – I know you wanted him to get well, *nicht?* You are new here. – the first child you see dying this way?

*(***GRETCHEN*** nods.)*

Look, it's hard to keep professional distance with such a helpless little thing…breaks the heart, I know.

*(***FRAU*** moves away.)*

This sort of thing still sometimes breaks mine –

GRETCHEN. But –

FRAU DIREKTORIN. I didn't think he was so sick either. But we all *must adjust!* ACCEPT! This is the way it is now. It will grow easier for you over time…accepting –

(silence)

GRETCHEN. *(whispering)* It's very hard –

FRAU DIREKTORIN. Try to think of it as I am trying: a *blessing* for the child – wherever the mother has taken him – if he goes fast –

GRETCHEN. Still –

FRAU DIREKTORIN. *(trying to convince herself:)* He would have suffered – helpless – in pain – years and years – like a little lame bird with broken wings –

(She moves away gaining complete control, turning back:)

They have shown me – statistics – graphs – he is already *"Der Nutzlose Esser"* – "A Useless Eater." They have shown me he and those like him are already *heavily* burdening The State. It will only grow worse, and we all *must help* rebuild the Greater Germany now, Fräulein! Use our resources to care for the healthy – those who can help the cause of the fatherland!

(Silence. They look at each other. Then:)

FRAU DIREKTORIN. *(cont.)* Burn the sheets – cleanse the room of him? It will be easier to forget that way.

(She sees **GRETCHEN** *not moving.)*

Now…? Please…?

(She turns, hurries out. **GRETCHEN**, *looks sadly at crib. Beat. Pulls self together, not allowing herself to sympathize anymore. She throws back shoulders, pulls off sheet, exits.* **ANGELIKA** *rises, moves from shadows:)*

ANGELIKA. *(to* **LUDMILLA***)* I've buried Little Hans on *Grossmutter*'s farm in the country, Ludmilla. I've written Carl it was natural causes – I can't bear to tell him what really happened here –

*(***ANGELIKA** *sinks down on stool, head down.* **LUDMILLA** *puts up sign.)*

("TO SAVE ONE LIFE IS TO SAVE THE WORLD")

LUDMILLA. *(to audience) Aber* Angelika is reported right away: "Kidnapper of The State Ward: Little Hans!" So, Angelika's scared *und* stays on her *Grossmutter*'s farm rocking Hansy's Teddy Bear like it's Hans, *und* he ain't dead!

*(***ANGELIKA** *sitting with Teddy, reading book:)*

ANGELIKA. "Now once upon a time," Hansy, "There were three bears – "

LUDMILLA. *(Shaking head. To audience)* Reading stories, *jetzt? Und* final straws? Starting conversations *mit* the Teddy Bear!

ANGELIKA. *(to Bear) Mutti* loves you, *liebes Kind*! You want your ginger cake, Hansy? And a sweater, *ja*? To keep you warm?

LUDMILLA. *Und* days passes – *und* this entire happening is getting more stranger than before!

ANGELIKA. You want Mutti to rub Hansy's sore tummy from that bad – med – medicine they – they – made you swallow down – ?? Want *Mutti* to be with you – take care of you always? You lonesome for *Mutti? Mutti*'s so sad, Hansy – so *lonely* she can't be here anymore without you – *GOTT? GOTT?*

(A beat. She looks at LUDMILLA.*)*

ANGELIKA. *(cont.) Gott's* not there! If there was *Gott* – would He have let this happen??

(She moves away, looks skyward.)

YOU AREN'T THERE! OLD WIVES TALES IS ALL YOU ARE!

(Rips cross from neck, throws to ground, takes pills from pocket,whispering skyward:)

At Church they say you burn in Hell for this but... HELL IS HERE NOW!

(Pours pills into hand. LUDMILLA *runs to her, trying to wrench pills from her hand.)*

LUDMILLA. Hey – hey – Angelika – give Ludmilla these rotten pills – ? Hey!

*(*ANGELIKA *runs from her.)*

ANGELIKA. Stay away from me!

LUDMILLA. Hey – you – you still got your Carl. He's your family now. You gonna make him suffer more losing you? When he suffers his baby gone *und* he's alone – gone with the Wehrmacht? You being sorry on *yourself.* Fiddling around *mit* devil pills??

(She advances on her.)

Give Ludmilla these pills! GIVE THEM TO ME!!

*(*ANGELIKA *runs farther away.)*

ANGELIKA. Leave me alone!

LUDMILLA. How I'm supposed to "leave you alone"? One of us going cuckoo is plenty enough, *ja?* Give me them devil pills! NOW!

*(*LUDMILLA *puts arm around* ANGELIKA, *with other hand wrenches away pills.* ANGELIKA *sobs on* LUDMILLA*'s shoulder.)*

LUDMILLA. *(cont.)* Hey – a brainstorm coming into my head: you been a religious girl – *Und* – I betcha, I betcha – you gonna be a religious girl in future events. For example: does camels lose their humps?

*(**LUDMILLA** picks up cross, slowly softly drapes it around **ANGELIKA**'s neck.)*

Gott gonna be *your* Big Helper – like he always was! All you gotta do is pray how you needs to get strong *und* brave on account of such a complete catastrophe happened to you, you can't be on top of any worlds right now unless *Gott* is helping you!

*(Beat. **ANGELIKA** now touches cross. Another beat before She crosses herself. **LUDMILLA** still holding her.)*

Hey – hey – more brain storms blowing in *mein* head! Listen: 100% Doctors *und* nurses is gone in the army! Nobody *here* a hundred miles in a circle to help sick peoples. *Mutters* expecting? Sick *Kinder*? Old peoples *mit* strokes. Nobody don't know nothing to do –

(Another beat. She looks at her. Softly)

So – could be a chance – maybe *you* –

ANGELIKA. I – I'm not strong enough Ludmilla –

LUDMILLA. Because you not eating *nothing*! *Brot!* Milk! Cheese! Eat *und* you gonna feel strong! *Und* not be no little girl at *Grossmutter's* crying on the past no more! We gonna have here instead – a big, brave strong nurse going taking care of sick peoples.

ANGELIKA. I – I haven't nursed for years –

LUDMILLA. But nursing? Like riding a bike! Nobody is forgetting how! Betcha – betcha – you could make *somebody* feel better – not batting your eyes. If you are having a clinic or something.

ANGELIKA. A – a clinic – ?

LUDMILLA. *Ja, ja!* Perfect. On account lots of people could come.

ANGELIKA. *My own* – ?

LUDMILLA. Why not?

ANGELIKA. A place where *everybody* could get help?

(laughing softly)

I – I used to dream of that when I was a girl –

LUDMILLA. So? Now you not a dreaming girl! You a big nurse!

ANGELIKA. But there's no place to have a clinic now – everything's crowded – people doubling up – War is coming –

*(**LUDMILLA** thinks, gets idea:)*

LUDMILLA. Weissbergen!

ANGELIKA. Weissbergen?

LUDMILLA. *Mein* final brainstorm: next village – you could bike there – take a look – an empty old house – west – off the square. Nobody been there in years – falling apart for example.

(She laughs.)

But peoples could help you fix her up –

*(**ANGELIKA** takes a deep breath, rises, turns apron, scarf to white nurse's side.)*

ANGELIKA. I'm going to take a look – Weissbergen! Maybe – maybe it would make do –

*(She takes bike goes to shadows as **LUDMILLA** goes back to her area, puts up sign:*

*(**"PRESERVING BEAUTIFUL THINGS"**)*

*(Sound of much glass shattering. **LUDMILLA** sits as **FRAU FÜHRERIN** comes forward from shadows, looks toward red glow growing brighter on scrim, smiles, walks toward red glow, disappearing in shadows in new direction, as sound of glass again in mixed with chanting: "Juden 'Raus, Juden 'Raus!" On scrim red glow grows brighter. **GRETCHEN**, hearing nothing, comes to balcony area. She is more cocky, more military – pins, insignias, etc draping festooned Nazi flag. Distant sounds continue: shattering glass, voices that then fade out.)*

GRETCHEN. *(calling to* **LUDMILLA,** *bragging:)* Berlin! The heart of everything! And? My *first* day – my brand new job: *Konsultantin* For "Frauenwerk"! Assisting Frau Führerin, The Chief Administrator!

LUDMILLA. *Ja?*

GRETCHEN. *(bragging even more)* She alone now controls *every* women's group in the country for the Reich! And *me?* I have *money!* A place of my own with a view! A NEW CAR. I will travel everywhere for Frau Führerin! Training group leaders and young girls – indoctrinating *all Frauen* of Germany: "You are the most beautiful," The most important women in the world! *Übermenschen:* blond – blue eyed – slim – and tall! The purest of Aryan stock! You –"

(Something attracts **GRETCHEN** *in the distance. To* **LUDMILLA***:)*

ACH GOTT! The Führer? There? Unannounced and slipping out of Berlin?

*(***GRETCHEN** *takes Nazi flag, waving it, calling:)*

Mein Führer! Mein Führer!

*(***GRETCHEN**, *entranced, a sensual yearning. To self:)*

I think he looked my way –

(She holds flag to face. Smells it, kisses it.)

Held me in his gaze! He looked through me! He knows me now!

(Looks off again whispers to Führer, confidentially.)

I love you, *mein Führer!* I submit completely! *Anything* you ask? I bow and do! All ARYAN WOMEN – "*Übermenschen*"! We alone will give birth to the shining knights of THE MASTER RACE!"

*(***FRAU FÜHRERIN**, *comes from shadows, with small fancy, white wrought iron scrollwork birdcage with two stuffed white birds inside. Also she carries a small string shopping bag.)*

GRETCHEN. *(cont.) (calling)* I think I just saw The Führer's motorcade going by –

FRAU FÜHRERIN. I saw nothing. I come from the other direction.

GRETCHEN. You don't go home then?

FRAU FÜHRERIN. Too tricky a night to get through. Safer here in the office. I even had to take the side streets to get back from there.

(She comes to **GRETCHEN**.*)*

GRETCHEN. Where?

*(*****FRAU*** *looks at her.)*

FRAU FÜHRERIN. Jewtown. You have been inside working the entire day and didn't see? Or hear the glass break?

GRETCHEN. What?

FRAU FÜHRERIN. Windows are all shattered and the whole Jewtown *burns!* Many fires. You can even see them from here –

(She's smiling, removes jacket, has sexy blouse beneath. She comes closer to **GRETCHEN** *who feels slightly uncomfortable and runs in direction of huge, red glow, smoke twisting up. This terrifies her.)*

GRETCHEN. I – I never saw such a thing before –

FRAU FÜHRERIN. *(Slight smiles crosses her lips again. Still closer to* **GRETCHEN**.*)* Well – I will tell you of many things you have never seen happen in Jewtown before. Our people's rage at the *Yid* explodes tonight! They smash glass all over – with stones – bricks – bullets – Jewtown windows shattered – homes – stores wide open –

*(*****GRETCHEN*** *sensing something, pulls away from* **FRAU**, *goes to cage.)*

GRETCHEN. *(forced laughter)* You have here birds?

FRAU FÜHRERIN. Stuffed doves. "Love birds" from "Feinstein's Bridal Shop"

GRETCHEN. You bought them?

FRAU FÜHRERIN. They were in the bridal window display
– but the window glass is shattered – So? I saw this
beautiful cage with love birds sitting there – I saved
them to preserve them.

GRETCHEN. *(surprised)* Herr Feinstein is not there to preserve them himself?

FRAU FÜHRERIN. *(chuckling)* Only looters.

*(FRAU again comes close to GRETCHEN, hand on her
shoulder. GRETCHEN more wary of FRAU, uncomfortable, breaks away to grocery bag.)*

GRETCHEN. And in here?

(She begins pulling things out.)

FRAU FÜHRERIN. *Brot und* Cheese – from Cohen's Delika-
tessen! *Und* from Goldmann's Liquors? The best vodka
there is!

(GRETCHEN looks at her, FRAU pulls out liquor bottle.)

I preserved everything!

GRETCHEN. *(moves farther away)* I – I never tasted vodka –

(She turns away.)

FRAU FÜHRERIN. *(looking hard at her) Ja.* Well –

*(FÜHRERIN looks at her as GRETCHEN move further
away.)*

FRAU FÜHRERIN. So. What bothers you?

GRETCHEN. I – I was never told the Reich gave permission
to our people for such violence! Smashing windows
– looting – setting *fires* –

FRAU FÜHRERIN. The *Yid* burns all of Jewtown himself.

GRETCHEN. WHAT?

FRAU FÜHRERIN. Runs in his synagogue to hide – mixes
his strange potions of Christian babies blood…Gets
drunk – careless! Lights his candles to Satan. Then?
The candles?

*(She comes close again, arm around GRETCHEN in
some way.)*

FRAU FÜHRERIN. *(cont.)* They catch fire on his rotting synagogue drapes – *Und?* The fire naturally spreads – through all Jewtown it spreads...

GRETCHEN. *(Scared. Of fire glow; looking at birdcage, groceries – the Frau)* And the looting?

FRAU FÜHRERIN. *(shakes head "no")* The SS has gone to bring order...calm the people's rage...

GRETCHEN. But the party has caused the peoples rage!

(She tries to break away but **FRAU** *keeps hold of her, growing angry.)*

FRAU FÜHRERIN. I have just told you how it is!

*(***FRAU*** *looks reproachfully at her. Silence.* **GRETCHEN** *can't move from* **FRAU***'s hold now.)*

You understand me?

GRETCHEN. *Nein –*

(She breaks away. Another silence. **FRAU** *looks at* **GRETCHEN** *who turns farther away. More silence, then* **FRAU** *comes back to her:)*

FRAU FÜHRERIN. You are rising very quickly, Fräulein. A beautiful, smart young person like you could move herself into top circles with Party Officers – in a year, maybe less. Meet important men – women –

(She moves close behind **GRETCHEN***.)*

And grows up!

*(***FRAU*** *takes hold of her shoulders.)*

Proves herself 100% Nazi! 200%!

GRETCHEN. But we've encouraged the violence, haven't we?

(Still behind her, **FRAU** *grips* **GRETCHEN***'s shoulders tighter, presses her to her body so* **GRETCHEN** *can't move.* **GRETCHEN** *is frightened now.* **FRAU** *speaks into* **GRETCHEN***'s ear.)*

FRAU FRUHRERIN. You will never *think* in that way again, Fräulein. That is dissent. Unpatriotic! You must think *only* the way of the Reich. Loyalty, Obedience, and Duty – if you want to rise.

GRETCHEN. I – I will try –

*(**GRETCHEN**, terrified, tries to release herself, can't.)*

But – please? I want –

FRAU FÜHRERIN. *(interrupting)* You will *do* it!

GRETCHEN. *Ja, ja.* Well. Now I will be going home then ...

*(A pause. **FRAU** still holding **GRETCHEN** from behind, slides hands down **GRETCHEN**'s breasts.)*

FÜHRERIN. You will stay all through the night too.

*(**GRETCHEN** throws her a look, starting to realize everything.)*

It is not safe for you to leave. We have even cheese and bread. And vodka.

GRETCHEN. *(whispering)* Please – don't make me do *that* – ? Let me go home – ? I'll do whatever else you say – but I – I'm – I'm not *that* way – please?

*(A silence. **FRAU** now lets her go, moves around in front of her, a little distance away. She stands looking at her.)*

FRAU FÜHRERIN. So. You will learn! *Hineingehen…*go in…

*(**GRETCHEN** makes a terrifying decision. The breath goes out of her. She stands limp, head down, completely submissive. Then moves to shadows. **FÜHRERIN** watches her, takes birdcage.)*

Und – we will find a perfect place for our beautiful love birds, *ja?*

*(She moves to shadows where **GRETCHEN** is, as **FRIEDERIKE** appears, calling in stage whisper to **LUDMILLA**:)*

FRIEDERIKE. I've got special news for Franz, Ludmilla –

*(**FRIEDERIKE** waves, looking into distance at Franz, Whispering to him;)*

Franz – Franz I'm expecting! He'll be born in Holland! FREE!

(Beat. To self:)

He's pulling back from me? Cringing?

(listens to Franz a moment, then:)

"We can't get out with you *that* way"???

(whispering to Franz:)

End the pregnancy?

LUDMILLA. *(to audience)* She is wanting this baby bad, I betcha, I betcha!

FRIEDERIKE. *(to Franz)* Our precious child and all I'll have left if –

(dogs BARKING)

Dogs! DOGS!

(BARKING, closer)

Run! FRANZ? RUN!

(MACHINE GUN, BARKING. **FRIEDERIKE** *screams, runs out. Silence. Then shocked:)*

LUDMILLA. *(to audience)* THEY KILLED FRANZ!

(blackout)

End of Act I

ACT TWO

*(***OBERAUFSEHERIN*** *and* **GRETCHEN** *enter on balcony.* **OBERAUFSEHERIN** *addressing Villageers In Village Squre:)*

OBERAUFSEHERIN. War is declared! This morning the warmongers France and Britain declared war on The Fatherland! We will not tolerate this aggression! We will defend our people *und* our land and demolish these aggressors! We will establish the master race in the thousand year Reich! *Sieg Heil!*

(She and **GRETCHEN** *give salute, exit.* **FRIEDERIKE**, *listening to radio, snaps it off, running to* **LUDMILLA**, *at her table.)*

FRIEDERIKE WAR, Ludmilla! We're at war! WAR! Goebbels just announced it on the radio. I've got to disappear – but how? I'll be showing soon – so Holland's out! And I have no legitimate papers! We're *all* are caught in the Nazi web – you know that? *Nothing*'s private now – everyone's spying – reporting on everyone else! The Gestapo's bursting in everywhere – searching papers, files, letters – listening to phone calls – taking away *anyone* they call "suspicious"! *Gott!* HELP ME?

(Silence. **LUDMILLA** *thinking, then:)*

LUDMILLA. I got it!

*(***LUDMILLA*** *puts up sign:)*

("FINDING WAYS AND MEANS")

(confidentially:)

A nurse is setting up a clinic next Village. Just starting in – plenty rooms – not no party member – *und* she don't got no help – besides you worked in a clinic once – Frau Nurse Angelika – Weissbergen – I'll get word to her –

61

FRIEDERIKE. I'll find her –

> *(**FRIEDERIKE** runs off as **GRETCHEN** appears with whip, dressed more militarily. **GRETCHEN** is now **AUF-SEHERIN**, she has changed. Haughtier, more arrogant, much colder. She comes from balcony area, stands back to audience, edge of proscenium.)*

LUDMILLA. *(to audience)* You know what? Now we got some-kinda little "Sub Work Camp" right outside the Village. *Und* they's marching prison womens down the Village street by *mein* bakery every morning six o'clock. Womens working like a dray horse out there fixing the street for army trucks. Not supposed to know what's going on? So what we got out there cold *und* thin like sticks *und* doubled over in pain? Ballerinas practicing? *Und* on top? A lady guard is *KLOPPING* them on their backs!

> *(**LUDMILLA** looks to where **GRETCHEN** now an **AUF-SEHERN** stands. She rises, puts crumbs in apron skirt, and holding up skirt, moves into scene going closer to **GRETCHEN** looking at her as **GRETCHEN** turns 3/4 back to **LUDMILLA**.)*

Hey – hey, Guard? I remember you! You are from here, *nicht?* I know you! I even know your whole family! The Schullers? Good Lutheran Germans once?

GRETCHEN. *Ja, ja.* Still.

LUDMILLA. You're the big sister?

GRETCHEN. *Ja, ja.*

LUDMILLA. So, listen, sister: *Mein Mutter* made so many *Kinder* for Hitler, we got in our house The Bronze, The Silver, *und* The Gold! But *Mutter* in a total paralysis! I raise all the *Kinder! Und* run The Bakery too, *ja?*

> *(**GRETCHEN AUFSEHERIN** nods, just slightly.)*

So –

> *(She starts sprinkling crumbs from apron, as if for birds.)*

I got here *mein* old stale bread crumbs. Throwing them on the Village street by our bakery. For birds, squirrels

– anything happens to come by. So – you wouldn't stop nothing when it's happening to come by, sister? I betcha – I betcha?

(Silence. To audience)

LUDMILLA. *(cont.)* She don't answer!

(mischievously)

But is getting nervous what I'm saying, *ja*?

*(She chuckles. Then to **GRETCHEN***:)*

Understand me, sister? We Dietrichs is good Germans! Good peoples still! So? How can us Dietrichs let starving womens come right by our Bakery *und* can't eat our stale crumbs? Could you Schullers?

*(She sprinkles more crumbs. **GRETCHEN AUFSEHERN** takes a step away.)*

So – you can't turn to me, sister Schuller? *Ja*? Then turn away some more! Tell the truth? *Give* me your back!

*(**GRETCHEN AUFSEHERN** turns back more, steps farther away, looking at sky.)*

GRETCHEN. *(between her teeth)* Remember I saw nothing – nothing –

LUDMILLA. *Ach,* sister, you don't see nothing!

(to audience)

On account she don't want to look!

*(She sprinkles crumbs until skirt's empty, runs back to stool, sitting as **FRIEDERIKE** comes forward calling to **ANGELIKA***:)*

FRIEDERIKE Nurse Angelika? Nurse Angelika?

*(**ANGELIKA** comes for an area in her clinic.)*

Frau Ludmilla sent me –

ANGELIKA. *Ja* –

FRIEDERIKE. Take me? Hide me? Let me nurse the sick with you?

ANGELIKA. But you carry a Gypsy's child! If they find you here – The Clinic's finished – we'd both be sent to a camp.

FRIEDERIKE. I'll wear a big nurse's apron so no one knows I'm pregnant! You have extra rooms to hide in – I'll stay there 'til night –

(Silence. She turns to her:)

I – I've nowhere else –

(Silence. ANGELIKA turns to her. They look into each other's eyes.)

Please?

ANGELIKA. Give me time to think –

(They walk different directions into shadows as:)

LUDMILLA. *(to audience)* So? What do you think about Johann *und* me?

(giggling, ecstatically happy)

We is *married! Ja, ja!*

(holds up wedding ring she wears)

A big, gold ring – both our initials and wedding date carved on the inside. *Und* – we had the best, most special Dietrich wedding cake ever gonna happen in the entire Germany! Five layers! 50 roses! Served the whole entire Village, my cake!

(ANGELIKA comes from shadows.)

ANGELIKA. Friederike?

(FRIEDERIKE appears, looking at ANGELIKA.)

This will be your home. We'll be together in this now!

FRIEDERIKE. I will never let you down!

(They embrace.)

ANGELIKA. *Willkommen! Willkommen!* I am happy you are here!

(FRIEDERIKE looks around:)

FRIEDERIKE. What can I do to help?

ANGELIKA Everything must be unpacked – sorted – put away – sheets, towels, medical supplies –

(**FRIEDERIKE** *begins unpacking items from baskets.*)

And all the medicines – there – and there – ? Sorted in the cupboard – quinine – aspirin – cough syrup –

(*They begin folding, stacking, storing items. Silence.* **FRIEDERIKE** *then looking at* **ANGELIKA**, *coming close:*)

FRIEDERIKE. (*confidential, whispering:*) Angelika – something else – ?

ANGELIKA. *Ja?*

FRIEDERIKE. I have a radio where I can get the BBC –

(*She pulls out radio.* **ANGELIKA** *frightened at this dangerous admission.*)

ANGELIKA. BBC? *Verboten!* We can't listen! Only the government network. Someone could come to the Clinic – and hear – and report us! Get rid of it! Quick! You haven't even got legitimate papers! I'm taking a risk with you as it is!

FRIEDERIKE. I'll hide it under my pillow – no one but me will hear –

ANGELIKA. I don't want to know anything about it! NOTHING! Why do you even tell me this?

(*Silence. Then:*)

FRIEDERIKE. I thought we were together in everything …

(*silence*)

ANGELIKA. It all scares me, Friederike.

FRIEDERIKE. There's one more thing?

ANGELIKA. What's that?

FRIEDERIKE. (*dropping to whisper:*) I've been told people are in hiding everywhere here – cellars, attics – holes in the ground – in the woods. Most are sick – and starving – living on bark and leaves and grass –

ANGELIKA. (*looking at her:*) Who?

FRIEDERIKE. Jews – Gypsies – homosexuals – dissenters – mentally disturbed or retarded – and the handicapped!

(Both now whisper through scene:)

We have to help them, Angelika –

(Silence. **ANGELIKA** *pacing. Then:)*

ANGELIKA. Dissent against the Reich like that? That's more than the radio – or the baby – we'll be executed on the spot.

(a beat)

FRIEDERIKE. How can *you* of all people say no?

ANGELIKA. It's *too* dangerous, Friederike.

FRIEDERIKE. Everything's dangerous! One way or the other – our very lives are only gambles now. Don't you see that? You have to trust in God.

(Silence. **ANGELIKA** *looks at her, holds her cross, pacing around.)*

How – how would they know where we are?

FRIEDERIKE. I'll bike into the woods nights. I know two, three signals. If I see or hear any signal coming back – any movement – I'll drop loaves of bread stuffed with directions to the clinic – I learned to do this before.

(beat)

ANGELIKA. Well – they – they'd have to come after hours –

FRIEDERIKE. On their own, I'll say – slip in that cellar door – give a password to us –

(Silence. Then:)

ANGELIKA. All right – all right – all right.

*(***LUDMILLA*** *hearing this, rises from stool, looking around to see if anyone sees her. She's frightened but determined. Puts shawl overhead.* **FRIEDERIKE** *goes into shadows.* **ANGELIKA** *goes to table, counts pills into bottle for verboten patients,* **LUDMILLA** *timidly enters scene without knocking.* **ANGELIKA** *turns, surprised, slides pills into pocket.)*

ANGELIKA. *(cont.)* I am sorry, the clinic's closed – ? I've had no special *word* – ?

(Beat. **ANGELIKA** *looks to see if she'll give the password signal she's a verboten patient.)*

That anyone was coming, I mean – after *normal hours?* The only time they're able to come?

*(***LUDMILLA*** *still gives no signal.)*

Well then – tomorrow morning. We open 8 o'clock.

*(***ANGELIKA*** *turns away, rolling bandages.)*

Guten Abend!

*(***LUDMILLA*** *starts out, stops.)*

LUDMILLA. *(shyly)* But Frau Nurse Angelika?

*(***ANGELIKA*** *whirls around, surprised again: she's still there.)*

ANGELIKA. *Ja?*

LUDMILLA. Johann Hecht?

ANGELIKA. *Ja?*

LUDMILLA. Our Bakery Delivery boy?

ANGELIKA. *Ja?*

(She looks quizzically, warily at **LUDMILLA**. *Silence,* **LUDMILLA** *mustering courage to speak. Then:)*

LUDMILLA. *(bursting out)* But see? I got 9 *Brudders und Schwesters* –

(Beat, **ANGELIKA** *very wary: Is she a spy? Decides to go along like a loyal Nazi.)*

ANGELIKA. *(managing a little smile)* So. Very patriotic. The Mutter's Bronze *and* Silver *and* Gold Cross in your house!

LUDMILLA. But *Mutti* can't even move now from all the *Kinder.* And Papa got a heart problem from worrying. All the work is mine.

ANGELIKA. Well – a loyal daughter to your *Mutti* and papa – and the Reich.

(She turns, rolling bandages, hoping **LUDMILLA** *will leave.* **LUDMILLA** *starts out, musters courage. Stops.)*

LUDMILLA. Frau Nurse –

*(***ANGELIKA*** startled again turns around.)*

ANGELIKA. *Ja?*

LUDMILLA. Johann? He just married me! *Und* we love each other. *Und* don't got so much things make us laugh and feel good except we got each other. *Und* I want him – *und* he wants me bad!

(pause)

ANGELIKA. *Ja,* well – you *are* married.

LUDMILLA. But I got to raise Mama's *Kinder* – *und* twins is in my family. So we can't take no chances having our own *Kinder.*

(Beat. She's close to tears.)

See – Johann he's going by the army any minutes. *Und* what I'm gonna do alone with *Mutti's Kinder* – *und* our own *Kinder?* *Und* run the bakery to support everybody all by myself? Hardly no money a soldier gets. So Johann decides he ain't by me in bed – is sleeping on a chair! So – how you tell your husband going to War "good-bye *mit* love" he on a chair?

(She is near tears.)

You got something maybe is helping me??

(a silence)

ANGELIKA. What are you asking me to do? *Birth control?* You know the law now forbids *anything* to stop childbirth.

LUDMILLA. Look – let everybody think it's for something else – and an operation I would be willing...

ANGELIKA. I would go to a camp for that...*verboten!*

(Silence. **LUDMILLA** *grows confidential, whispering.)*

LUDMILLA. But I hear you are helping many peoples who's *verboten* – problems happening to them ...?

(Silence. **ANGELIKA** *feels danger, doesn't like what* **LUDMILLA** *knows:)*

ANGELIKA. The people who come to this clinic, are all registered villagers, Frau. And sick. You are not sick. You have a choice – I cannot help you.

*(***ANGELIKA*** slowly raises her arm in Nazi salute.)*

Heil Hitler!

LUDMILLA. *(reluctantly saluting) Heil Hitler!*

(She goes to stool, sits. To audience)

A simple country woman, *ja*? And Johann? A simple country man. Well. So. things are *schlecht*. Bad! *Und* what is happening to anybody's life? For example: you know what I am seeing? Good Dr. Ginsberg – the only Jew I know? They are chasing him with a whip down the street to a truck and taking him away! Bare naked with a sign on him: "*Ich bin Jude Ginsberg.*" *Ach!* I am hiding so he don't see me! I am ashamed! *And* scared!

(starts tearing bread on table into pieces)

I don't know. Do we know what we are doing?

(She keeps crumbling the bread.)

It's like we don't. We lost our minds or something.

(She puts crumbs in a bowl.)

It's like we are howling with the wolves!

*(***FRIEDERIKE*** comes from shadows, looking for **ANGELIKA**. She is in labor, stops to brace herself with each spasm. She moans, cries out, making her way across area.)*

FRIEDERIKE Angelika? Angelika? It's coming – IT'S COMING!

(She moans with the spasm as **ANGELIKA** *comes quickly, puts arms around her, as* **LUDMILLA** *watches.)*

ANGELIKA. Don't worry! You and the baby will be safe.

*(***ANGELIKA*** helps her lay down, sits beside her, both obscured. **LUDMILLA** happy, to audience:)*

LUDMILLA. So? Johann? Changed his mind on the predicaments he's been cooking up concerning chairs –

(She smiles, embarrassed.)

Three times we in the bed! *Und* then he goes – *Und* then – nine months is going by – *und* what you could imagine we are getting?

(Proudly she holds up baby in basket in one hand.)

GRISELDE!

(She holds up second baby in basket, ever more proud, swinging baskets.)

Und CHRIMELDE!

(She laughs.)

Ja, ja! We do! We do!

*(**ANGELIKA** comes from obscured area handing baby to **FRIEDERIKE**.)*

It's a healthy little girl, Friederike.

*(She crosses herself, gives basket to **FRIEDERIKE** who kisses baby in basket.)*

FRIEDERIKE. *(to baby)* FRANZISKA I name you! So now – through all time your Papa lives!

ANGELIKA. We'll all live in my private rooms, *Ja?* So *nobody* knows she came. When she is up, you stay with her there. When she sleeps, you help me.

FRIEDERIKE. *Ja…ja…*

ANGELIKA. At night you can bring her out in the clinic rooms.

*(They sit in shadows, obscured, as **LUDMILLA** to audience)*

LUDMILLA. So – now I got Griselde *und* Chrimelde *und* Johann's at the front. *Und* Mama *and* Papa? Gone! Six months apart! . *Und* how can I do everything alone? *Gott im Himmel!* I wish we are *winning* already so Johann comes home!

(She comes closer.)

Then – *meine cousine* Hedi comes to me. Her *mann* Otto is gone to War too. *Und* she's got *Kinder* too. So we decide we gonna live together – keeping the little farm, the bakery *und* the *Familie* together.

(She chuckles.)

Keeping each other together too! *Nicht?*

(She laughs. GRETCHEN *[*AUFSEHERIN*] comes forward, toward* LUDMILLA *who sees her.)*

Aber – why do we got the government in on it too? I got to sell *our* stuff to them! *Und* they don't pay NOTHING! *Und* they are *keeping track* on everything what we got!

*(*GRETCHEN *comes to her, looking at clipboard.)*

GRETCHEN. You are keeping here an even dozen geese, Frau Ludmilla?

LUDMILLA. *Ja, ja.*

GRETCHEN. So. We are expecting you deliver 48 eggs.

LUDMILLA. *Ja, ja.*

GRETCHEN. And you've got here three nanny goats giving milk and cheese?

LUDMILLA. *Ja,* we do.

GRETCHEN. So – your quota is eight quarts of milk – 2 pounds of cheese

LUDMILLA. *Ja.*

GRETCHEN. *(saluting) Sieg Heil!*

LUDMILLA. *(saluting) Sieg Heil!*

*(*GRETCHEN *exits up through arch.* LUDMILLA *sits on stool.)*

(to audience. With glee) Hey? You know what? I am finagling! *Ja, ja!*

(As she tells this to audience, she grows more confidential:)

LUDMILLA. *(cont.)* Shh? On account: there is rich German
city *Frauen* – close by Berlin – in their castles hundreds
of years their families is so rich? But they can't get no
food! So what do you think? Castles near the city and
has beautiful things? They is coming *here* in secret!
Wants to trade what beautiful things they got for food.
Und why not? I got food but ain't got no beautiful
things!

(Still giggling, She picks up basket, with a goose.)

See? I got *mein* number *thirteen* goose – Gertrud! Which
I gave her the name! *Ja, ja, I did! Und* they don't figure
out *mein* finagle on Gertrud on account she is sitting in
her nest in the cellar when they comes!

*(She chuckles, strokes goose, now pulls egg out, admiring
it in the light.)*

Und see what *she* is laying? GOLDEN EGGS – exact
kind like fairy tales. *Und* city womens is paying like
gold to get one!

*(She laughs more, smoothing Gertrud's feathers, then
puts egg in basket.)*

Ja. Well. Last? Best finagle? "NANKA"! *Mein* nanny
goat! Which I named her in addition! I did! I did!

(Laughs, then, as if Nanka arrives. LUDMILLA *nuzzles
her, coaxes her center, presenting her to audience.)*

Und the government don't know about Nanka neither
on account she's in the cellar too. *Und* I get plenty milk
und cheese from Nanka.

(roaring with laughter)

Ach! She is the smart goat! Don't "butt her head" on
the cellar wall. Don't bleat. Don't never make one
sound when they comes to "keep track" on me. *Und*
what you think? For our milk *und* cheese – Hedi and
me is getting wool, linen, silk to make Easter clothes
for the whole family entire. Then? We is pulling shut
our curtains so *nobody* sees our Easter table where we

got a big ham on a pure *Dresden* platter! *Und* silver spoons, *und* knives *und* forks! Know what Hedi says? "All we don't got now is an Oriental rug in the barn for the cows!"

(She is chuckling, walking to table:)

So. People has got to find a ways and means –

(Takes bowl, begins stirring, as **FRIEDERIKE***, with baby, crying in basket enters clinic, sits, hums. Baby is quiet. Puts baby on floor, rocking basket with her foot as* **OBER-AUFSEHERIN***,* **GRETCHEN** *[*AUFSEHERIN*] rush into clinic,* **OBERAUFSEHERIN** *screaming: "Festnehmen! Hineingehen!! Schnell!! SCHENLL!" as* **ANGELIKA** *enters, rushes to* **FRIEDERIKE***:)*

ANGELIKA. Get in the bedroom! Lock it! Quick! They're breaking in! HIDE HER!

FRIEDERIKE. *Ach Gott!* It's three in the morning. What's –

*(***OBERAUFSEHERIN***,* **GRETCHEN** *[*AUFSEHERIN*] stomp into area as* **FRIEDERIKE** *shoves baby basket behind chair with her foot.)*

OBERAUFSEHERIN. We have information someone here is associated with ESPIONAGE! And a non-Aryan, non-registered baby is crying here, middle of the night.

ANGELIKA. Such a story! Only my assistant – and me are here middle of the night.

OBERAUFSEHERIN. We will determine who is here! Search the rooms!

(Snaps fingers for **GRETCHEN** *to look.* **FRIEDERIKE** *thinks: the baby! She runs, gets radio, from a hiding place, wires dangling.)*

FRIEDERIKE. It was the BBC broadcasting middle of the night! I was listening secretly. That's what you heard.

(She gives radio to her.)

I have the associations with the Underground. The good Nurse knows nothing.

*(OBERAUFSEHERN looks at FRIEDERIKE, radio, ANGE-
LIKA, then around room. A long silence. She walks
slowly to ANGELIKA:)*

OBERAUFSEHERIN. There are *no* doctors or nurses in this
district for the people. So. No further measures are
taken now. At this time. But – we believe a baby is
here! We will return! *Sieg Heil!*

(She salutes.)

GRETCHEN. *Sieg Heil!*

(She salutes.)

ANGELIKA. *(forcing a salute) Sieg Heil!*

*(OBERAUFSEHERIN snaps fingers, GRETCHEN takes
radio, handcuffs FRIEDERIKE, who covertly nods towards
baby basket behind chair. ANGELIKA nods back subtly.)*

OBERAUFSEHERIN. *(to FRIEDERIKE)* You are now in
Protective Custody. Incarceration? Ravensbruck Concentration Camp for Women! The crime? "Preparation
for High Treason!" *Heraus! HERAUS!*

*(GRETCHEN pushes FRIEDERIKE away and through
arch as ANGELIKA picks up basket with baby.)*

ANGELIKA. *(softly to baby) Kleine Mädel, kleine Mädel –* Tante
Angelika will guard you with her life!

(She gets Teddy Bear.)

Your Teddy Bear, *liebes Kind! Ja, ja!*

(She crosses self, move to shadows with basket.)

LUDMILLA. *(to audience)* So – nobody finds Baby Franziska!
On account somebody always is getting word to Angelika when they is coming looking. These times? She
hides Franziska in the convent.

*(OBERAUFSEHERIN, wearing cape, military medals,
carrying whip,appears in new area: Concentration
camp, shoving FRIEDERIKE, handcuffed, before her.
FRIEDERIKE stumbles down to ground level, as AUF-
SEHERIN [GRETCHEN] in SS Camp Guard uniform
enters beside OBERAUFSEHERIN, both chuckling.)*

OBERAUFSEHERIN. *ACHTUNG!! ACHTUNG!!*

*(**FRIEDERIKE** pulls herself to attention, looks at **OBER-AUFSEHERIN**, who comes to edge of balcony, tapping crop handle against her side. **FRIEDERIKE** stands straighter. **OBERAUFSEHERIN** snaps fingers.)*

Weg nahmen!

*(**GRETCHEN** goes to **FRIEDERIKE**, removes her handcuffs, throws camp striped apron, striped scarf on ground.)*

Anziehen! Put it on!

*(**FRIEDERIKE** does. **GRETCHEN** sticks Red Triangle and a number on her shirt.)*

You will be trained for the plumbing detail! *Heraus! Heraus!*

*(**FRIEDERIKE** runs to shadows, crouching, **OBERAUF-SEHERIN** and **GRETCHEN** to shadows, other area.)*

LUDMILLA. *(to audience)* So. You know about this Womans' Camp Ravensbruck, *ja?* They are calling it "The Last Station." Why? The last station where the cattle train is stopping? And nobody goes to no other train station again? Or could be – "The Last Station of The Cross" – ?

(She puts up sign:)

("AT THE LAST STATION")

Fifty five miles only from Berlin. North.

*(She gives a deeply ironic laugh. It's turning night. **OBE-RAUFSEHERIN** appears in remote part of Camp. Leans against post, lights cigarette, as **GRETCHEN** [**AUFSEH-ERIN**] appears, not seeing her, sits, takes letter from pocket, holds it to her breast, happy, opens it, suddenly screams out as reads letter. **OBERAUFSEHERIN** turns, **GRETCHEN** sees her, calls to her, waving letter:)*

GRETCHEN. *Ach! Gott!* My baby brother, Klaus! He dies at the front*!*

(She's sobbing. **OBERAUFSEHERIN** *scrutinizes her coldly, doesn't come to her.)*

OBERAUFSEHERIN. You are off-limits, Frau Aufseherin! Head officers only. *Heraus!*

*(***GRETCHEN***, still sobbing, doesn't move.)*

GRETCHEN. I – I didn't think it will happen to him – I –

OBERAUFSEHERIN. What did you picture? He was attending maybe a Songfest in a beer garden? We are at *war!* Leave the area now!

(Beat. **GRETCHEN** *still doesn't rise. Then she speaks quietly:)*

GRETCHEN. He was the only brother –

*(***OBERAUFSEHERIN** *looks around, comes closer.)*

OBERAUFSEHERIN. All families sacrifice! This is the way it goes! *Two* brothers I have already lost! You have some special exemption? *Aufstehen!* Get up! Stop sniveling!

GRETCHEN. But –

OBERAUFSEHERIN. *(whispering) Mein Grossvater. Vater. Brudders!* All officers! All sacrificing their lives for the greater Germany. Take *pride!* This *Bruder* of yours dies a Hero – a Patriot – a Sacrifice for The Higher Cause!

GRETCHEN. *(blurting out:)* But his last leave? He wanted out! He said: "Our *own officers* are hanging us from trees if we complain one word! We're *losing the war!*"

OBERAUFSEHERIN. WE ARE WINNING THE WAR!!

GRETCHEN. He was *there!* He said we are losing!

(whispering, between her teeth:)

OBERAUFSEHERIN. *Treason!* And *you* are committing it now repeating his traitorous words! *Gehen Sie!*

*(***GRETCHEN** *overwhelmed with grief and not able to stop. She is sobbing, holds out snapshot.)*

GRETCHEN. *Mutter* sends me his only picture – it's all I have left of him – I –

(**OBERAUFSEHERIN** *takes picture, looks at it, crumples it with deliberateness.* **GRETCHEN**, *jumps to up get it. They struggle.*)

GRETCHEN. *Zurück geben! Zurück geben*! It's mine!

OBERAUSEHERIN. *HALT!*

(**GRETCHEN** *keeps struggling.*)

HÖREN SIE? HALT!

(**GRETCHEN** *lets go.* **OBERAUFSEHERIN** *takes cigarette to photo.*)

GRETCHEN. Don't! DON'T!

(*Photo catches fire.* **OBERAUFSEHERIN** *drops it to ground. Speaks impersonally, formally, for anyone to hear.*)

OBERAUFSEHERIN. You are off-limits here, Frau Aufseherin. Chief Officers only. Resume duties! *Schnell!*

(**OBERAUFSEHERIN** *retreats to shadows. A beat.* **GRETCHEN** *makes decision: deadly resolution. Throws letter on top of burning photo, stomps on burning letter, photo 'til they are ashes. Her last touch with her soul, anything personal:*)

GRETCHEN. '*Raus!* OUT! '*RAUS!*

(*Her face is cold stone. She is now only an Instrument of the State. She throws back shoulders, exits as* **LUDMILLA** *appears:*)

LUDMILLA. *(to audience, whispering)* So? Now? They are making a big tent in the camp like the circus – *und* Jew womans from Hungary is getting dumped in – no electricity – nothing – just some big tent on the bare earth –

FRIEDERIKE. *(whispering to* **LUDMILLA** *from shadows, as she watches)* Driving them in – stripping them naked – dogs biting them to pieces while they dump the women on the freezing ground – one on top of the other on top of the other –

(**FRIEDERIKE**, *head down, now rising from shadows, crosses area with plumbers kit, as* **OBERAUFSEHERIN & GRETCHEN AUFSEHERIN** *both with whips in belts, come into bright light on balcony. They're slightly high,* **OBERAUFSEHERIN** *swigging from bottle. Passes it to* **GRETCHEN** *who swigs too. She puts basket on table. They look down, see* **FRIEDERIKE**.)

OBERAUFSEHERIN. *(to* **GRETCHEN**) So? Now tonight prove you are 200% Nazi! Show me *how* you will give that *stuck* her Christmas cake from the Red Cross.

(**GRETCHEN** *taking dare with new boldness, takes cake from basket moves forward.*)

GRETCHEN. Stop, *stuck!*

FRIEDERIKE. *(Surprised they're there. Stopping.) Ja, Frau Aufseherin.*

GRETCHEN. *(holding up cake)* From The Red Cross. For Christmas. One cake for each *Stück.*

(taking bite of cake)

Mmm! Raisins – nuts – ginger spice! And you are hungry, *nicht*? Famished? Starving?

FRIEDERIKE. *Ja,* Frau Aufseherin

(**GRETCHEN** *takes another bite.*)

GRETCHEN. So. *Kommen Sie hier, Stück! Schnell!*

(**FRIEDERIKE** *puts down kit, comes close.*)

SPRINGEN! JUMP FOR IT!

(She tosses cake high in the air, in opposite direction from where **FRIEDERIKE** *stands.* **FRIEDERIKE** *jumps, misses, cake falls to floor as does* **FRIEDERIKE**. **GRETCHEN** *looks to* **OBERAUFSEHERIN** *as they laugh.*)

OBERAUFSEHERIN. You have nothing else to show me?

(**GRETCHEN** *thinks, takes the dare, goes down to where* **FRIEDERIKE** *is, smashes cake with her boot.*)

GRETCHEN. Dog food now, *ja?* –

(She looks at **OBERAUFSEHERIN** *who nods in approval, gets idea: throws down a belt.)*

OBERAUFSEHERIN. Leash her!

*(***GRETCHEN** *takes the dare, leashes* **FRIEDERIKE** *around neck. Laughs with* **OBERAUFSEHERIN**.*)*

GRETCHEN. Now? *Wie ein Hund!* Like a dog! ALL FOURS! Eat it! *ESSEN!* LICK!

(pushing **FRIEDERIKE** *to ground)*

*(***FRIEDERIKE***, on all fours like a dog, licks food from floor.* **GRETCHEN** *looks half smilingly to* **OBERAUF-SEHERIN** *who nods approval again, smiling too.)*

GRETCHEN. Now Bark! *Bellen!*

*(***FRIEDERIKE** *barks.* **GRETCHEN & OBERAUFSEHERIN** *laugh,* **FRIEDERIKE** *crawls into shadows, huddled up.* **GRETCHEN** *goes back to* **OBERAUFSEHERIN** *who holds up bottle:)*

OBERAUFSEHERIN. To my *kleine* 200% Nazi!

(They laugh, She drinks, passes bottle to **GRETCHEN**.*)*

So. Tonight you will distribute Red Cross cakes to the entire Block 7 in this way? All dogs! All barking! While I oversee the action, *ja?* Continuing to show me how 200% faithful, loyal and obedient you are!

GRETCHEN. *(cocky)* Why not?

OBERAUFSEHERIN. *Ja.* Well. Such a Fräulein deserves beautiful jewelery, *nicht?*

(From pocket she takes small box, opens it, shows it.)

GRETCHEN. Golden earrings!

*(***OBERAUFSEHERIN** *takes golden earrings puts them on* **GRETCHEN**.*)*

FRIEDERIKE. *(whispering to* **LUDMILLA***:)* It's *our* jewelry – stolen – and all our shoes – socks – coats – blankets. 20° in the bunks – and their storerooms? Stuffed to the ceiling with our Red Cross quilts –

(She crawls deeper into shadows, obscured. **GRETCHEN** *is striking dramatic poses in earrings.)*

OBERAUFSEHERIN. Beautiful! Beautiful!

(OBERAUFSEHERIN & GRETCHEN *move to Shadows.* **LUDMILLA** *looks around:)*

LUDMILLA. *(to audience) Und?* Now? Cousine Hedi delivering our 48 quota goose eggs there. But the Ravensbruck Kitchen Guard takes *meine* eggs *und* laughs *und* tells her he got some kind new order: "The Jew Tent pigs is getting cut to *one* vat dirty water! *One* raw beet! O*ne* time a day!" So who is getting nourishment there off *mein* golden eggs? HUH?

(FRIEDERIKE *creeps to new shadowy area watching. To* **LUDMILLA***:)*

FRIEDERIKE. Six days since they first dumped the women in the tent – and the dogs again! Driving half the women *back* on the trucks – and next day? More come – next day? More *go* –

LUDMILLA. *(to audience)* "To The Killing Centers," says the old village Grandpas who sit up all night *und* watch the dark road –

FRIEDERIKE. *(standing, watching:)* Truck after truck – night after night – all through the nights.

(She crouches in shadows as **ANGELIKA** *and* **LUDMILLA** *come from Shadows.)*

ANGELIKA. *(to* **LUDMILLA***)* I'm leaving Franziska hidden in the convent again, Ludmilla, with the nun I trust. I have to go to Berlin.

(She starts to another area.)

(LUDMILLA *puts up sign:)*

("SHELTERS FROM STORMS")

LUDMILLA. *(to audience)* She got a letter from the Wehrmacht? Her Carl's sick in a hospital in Berlin – but she don't know where so she got to go looking in the wards.

(**ANGELIKA** *disappears into shadows.*)

LUDMILLA. *Und* you know what? *Meine* Old *Tante* Uta living alone in Dresden. *Und* I can't take it with her there by herself! I want *meine Familie* together!

(**LUDMILLA** *rises. To audience*)

I got to get her from Dresden *und* bring her here!

(*She puts on shawl, enters scene, moving to another area.*)

Never been so far away from *meine Kinder und* Hedi's afraid for me to go. But I got to!

(*She keeps going.*)

Besides they are telling me Dresden is special: no industry. Only nice *und* old *und* pretty buildings. The Englishers is gonna leave Dresden alone, I betcha, I betcha! It is so safe they don't even got one bomb shelter or siren there!

(*She stops, looks around in awe:*)

Dresden! Beautiful!

(*moves to new area*)

Und Tante's ready to leave *und* goes to buy a new shawl to –

(**OBERAUFSEHERIN & AUFSEHERIN [GRETCHEN]** *enter in bright lights calling out [possibly with megaphones, siren, loud buzzer, overlapping:]*)

OBERAUFSEHERIN. DRESDEN! ENGLISHER BOMBERS!

GRETCHEN. BERLINERS! AMERICANER BOMBERS!

OVERAUFSEHERIN & GRETCHEN. (*overlapping*) *HERAUS ALLEN! HERAUS! OUT! DRESDENERS! BERLINERS! HERAUS! HERAUS!*

(*As sirens blare* **LUDMILLA** *whirls around, looking everywhere,* **ANGELIKA** *running from shadows, looking everywhere. To* **LUDMILLA***:*)

ANGELIKA. *GOTT!* I can't get to Carl –

(She runs. **ANGELIKA***'s following speeches to self:)*

Where's shelter?

LUDMILLA. *(Paralyzed. To audience) Tante's* not back. What should I do?

(SIREN SOUNDS LOUDER. She starts running)

OBERAUFSEHERIN.	**GRETCHEN.**
ALLEN HERAUS!	*BERLINERS! HERAUS!*
DRESDEN! OUT!	*HERAUS!!*
HERAUS!	

ANGELIKA. Everyone running – trampling me – CARL?

*(***LUDMILLA*** running, looking:)*

LUDMILLA. *Tante?*

(to audience)

All the peoples is screaming: "If Dresden goes, we go too!"

(looking around, calling:)

TANTE??

(bombs hitting)

ANGELIKA. A HIT! Screaming!

(She runs away. SIRENS LOUDER, LOUDER)

OBERAUFSEHERIN. ATTACK! ATTACK!

ANGELIKA. *(looking around:)* I'm trapped! Where's shelter? CARL?

LUDMILLA. *(looking around)* There's *no shelter*! *TANTE??*

(BOMBS)

GOTT! What would *MEINE KINDER* do something happens to me? I shouldn't a come I betcha, I betcha!

(BOMBS. She crouches, covering head with shawl. BOMB.)

ANGELIKA. It's hitting here! Homes flying up – crumbling – gingerbread!

(She whirls around. BOMB)

GOTT! IT'S HITTING!

(She crouches in shadows. BOMB)

LUDMILLA. IT HITS!

(BOMB)

ANGELIKA. IT HITS!

(BOMB)

TOGETHER IT HITS! IT HITS! IT HITS!

(Silence. **OBERAUFSEHERIN & GRETCHEN** *leave. Then:)*

ANGELIKA. Over? Peeping out –

LUDMILLA. Crawling – creeping – standing –

ANGELIKA. *(looking around)* Berlin? Ghost city – crater on the moon –

(She looks to sky: shooting flames, smoke twisting.)

Lightning flames – choking smoke –

(She clutches cross.)

GOTT! WHAT EVIL!

*(***LUDMILLA*** looking around.)*

LUDMILLA. *(to audience)* A big pile of ashes – Dresden. *Und Tante?* A bunch a charcoal bones? I betcha – I betcha.

(She's walking around, wrapped in shawl. Dazed, as is **ANGELIKA** *who keeps walking, looking.)*

ANGELIKA. *(to self:)* How can I find Carl…? Can't even walk – mud clumps – ashes – debris – *Gott!* Crushed up corpses, too – mixed into everything –

LUDMILLA. *(to audience)* Dead peoples stacked like wood… didn't do nothing but live here –

ANGELIKA. *(to self:)* Are pieces of Carl here – ?

(She stops, looking.)

LUDMILLA. They is BURNING THEM LIKE WOOD – SMELLS GETTING ME SICK AT MY STOMACH INSIDE!

ANGELIKA. Rib cage – eye – CARL??

LUDMILLA. *(to audience)* A little girl – crying for her dead *Mutti.* She picks something up. *"Frau?* A doll's head – burnt up black *und* smiling!" *Aber* I'm looking – *und* it ain't no doll's head – it's a baby's head burnt up – without no body!

(She is breaking down at this.)

(sight, screaming, looks to heaven)

GOTT! I don't know what I hate no more or why! But I hate! I never hate nothing, nobody in mein life. *Aber* – I HATE THE WAR! *UND* I HATE THE ENGLISH-ERS! I HATE THE AMERICANERS! *UND* I HATE *THE JEWS!*

(She puts her hands over her face sobbing into shawl.)

Und I can't help it! *Und* nobody can help it! We is all crying *und* cursing *und* blaming *them*! THEM! *THEM!!*

ANGELIKA. *(looking up to sky)* ARE WE IN THE REAL WORLD – OR WHERE?

*(**ANGELIKA** crosses herself. Both looking at sky, begin backing away:)*

TOGETHER. BURNINGBURNINGBURNING! BURNING-BURNINGBURNING!

*(**ANGELIKA** backs away into shadows, obscured. **LUD-MILLA** to her area, puts up sign:)*

("THE LORD GIVETH THE LORD TAKETH AWAY")
*(**FRIEDERIKE** on her way somewhere as **OBERAUF-SEHERIN** appears:)*

OBERAUFSEHERIN. Toilets stopping up! Stuck! Blocks 4, 5, 6, Repair it! *Mach schnell!*

FRIEDERIKE. *Ja*, Frau Oberaufseherin.

*(**OBERAUFSEHERIN** to shadows as **FRIEDERIKE** whis-pering to **LUDMILLA**:)*

The toilets for the camp are built above the big Tent
– where the drain enters. Everything flows from here.

(**FRIEDERIKE** *grabs pump, moves to another area.*)

So we decide to pump here. For a whole day we pump
and we pump – but it's not helping! More toilets are
stopping up!

(**OBERAUFSEHERIN** *comes forward.*)

OBERAUFSEHERIN. You take another day for this? Ten
women die for your laziness!

FRIEDERIKE. *(whispering to* **LUDMILLA***)* It's getting worse!
Head Plumber says stoppage is happening in one drain
after the other in an order. But where's the source?

(*She is looking one place then another.* **OBERAUFSEH-
ERIN** *comes forward.*)

OBERAUFSEHERIN. You GOSSIP?? Ten more women die!
Und twenty more lie naked, tied, ready to be whipped.
If by night the entire problem is not repaired? They
meet *their* fate!

(*She retreats.*)

FRIEDERIKE. *(whispering to* **LUDMILLA***)* Night's starting to fall
– almost too dark to see –

(*She stops pumping suddenly, stunned, whispers to* **LUD-
MILLA***:*)

No water in the last drain! By the tent! It's all clogged
up behind it – that's the source!

(*She listens where she's been pumping, then:*)

Gott! Now? Water's bubbling up from below! Something's come free down there!

(*pumping more:*)

Drain's open! More water's coming. Bubbling! Pour-
ing free! *GOTT!* It's fixed! *GOTT IM HIMMEL!*

(*Calling:*)

TELL THEM IT'S FIXED!

(She looks down the hole, whispering to **LUDMILLA**.*)*

FRIEDERIKE. *(cont.)* What – ? Water's drained – only refuse – but there's something light down there. A little rabbit?? That stopped it all up?

(She pulls up a bundle, stands silent, looking. Then looks up to balcony: **FRAU OBERAUFSEHERIN & AUF-SEHERIN [GRETCHEN]** *stand in shadows.* **FRIEDERIKE** *to* **LUDMILLA**)*

FRIEDERIKE. *(whispering)* A dead boy. Newborn, Ludmilla. A perfect Jewish boy from the tent. It's breaking my heart in two – as if he were *my* Franziska – So beautiful. All that muck, and *he's* white as snow – ?

(She looks toward **OBERAUFSEHERIN**, *not seeing her in shadows whispering to* **LUDMILLA**.*)*

They'll be coming in minutes! If they find *out*, they'll whip 30 more to death! I've got to dig a hole here. Bury him! Now!

(She digs, talks to self:)

Cover it – line it – something –

(She looks, grabs straw on ground.)

Straw!

*(***FRIEDERIKE** *covers hole with straw.)*

Rest safely now –

(She kisses spot where baby lies while **ANGELIKA** *with Franziska, comes from shadows, sits, rocking Franziska in her arms, as* **LUDMILLA** *rises, gets baskets with her two babies, holds one in arms, puts other who's in basket on floor, then sits rocking basket with her foot. In their various areas. The women feel the pain of the mother whose baby* **FREDERIKE** *found and they feel profound sadness of this death. They mourn together. First* **ANGE-LIKA** *sings "ALL THROUGH THE NIGHT" [German & Welsh lullaby].* **LUDMILLA & FRIEDERIKE** *hum. Next verse [in German] they sing together. Last verse together also. Can be variations on how this is done.)*

ANGELIKA.

> "Sleep my child and peace attend thee
> All through the night.
> Guardian angels God will send thee
> All through the night."

ALL.

> "*Schlaf mein Kind mit Freiden leben*
> *In stiller Nacht.*
> *Wachter Engel Gottes Beschutze Dich,*
> *In stiller Nacht.*"

> *(The **WOMEN** are in different areas, but united, as if together. **ANGELIKA** crosses self, looking skyward, as others do. Song lines below can be divided as they sing and hum:)*

FRIEDERIKE. *(praying to God)* Forgive us! For what has happened here, *Gott? GOTT? FORGIVE US ALL!!*

LUDMILLA. For saying nothing when they was putting Dr. Ginsberg on the truck…

ANGELIKA. For doing nothing to take Hans from that Clinic the first day we went –

> *(silence)*

FRIEDERIKE. *(whispering to God)* Please *Gott?* Bless this baby Jewish boy. He's nestled in the straw now – like little Baby Jesus…like your Chosen Son –

LUDMILLA. *Und* bless his poor Jewish Mama – like a Madonna –

ANGELIKA. Made to sacrifice *her* boy child at "The Last Station" of the cross –

LUDMILLA. *Und* let me never help this happen to no mother's newborn baby no more. Amen.

ANGELIKA. Amen.

> (**ANGELIKA** *crosses self.*)

FRIEDERIKE. Amen

LUDMILLA. *(singing now:)*

> THOUGH SAD FATE OUR LIVES MAY SEVER

ANGELIKA. *(singing:)*

PARTING WILL NOT LAST FOREVER

FRIEDERIKE. *(singing:)*

THERE'S A HOPE THAT LEAVES ME NEVER

ALL. *(singing:)*

ALL THROUGH THE NIGHT.

(They begin to move slowly to their shadowy areas, possibly singing:)

Star of faith the dark adorning. All through the night. Lead us fearless t'wards the morning. All through the night. Though our hearts be wrapt in sorrow, from the hope of dawn we borrow promise of a glad tomorrow – All through the night.

*(**LUDMILLA** at her table snaps off radio.)*

LUDMILLA. *(to audience)* So, now I hear Herr Clubfoot Goebbels "Complete Fairy Tale Hour" on the radio. Pretending it's news and we is *beating the Russians?* But *We* ain't beating no Russians! WE is the ones *Kapput!*

*(**LUDMILLA** puts up sign:)*

("THE BEGINNING OF THE END")

*(She mixes in bowl, as **FRIEDERIKE** comes forward from shadows, she is almost in a daze, dumbfounded, she is crouching, whispering to **LUDMILLA**:)*

FRIEDERIKE. Shh! – shh – Ludmilla – ?

LUDMILLA. *(whispers) Ja?*

*(A beat. **FRIEDERIKE**, looks around furtively. Whispering:)*

FRIEDERIKE. *(Can't believe what she's saying:)* Whispers snaking – mouth – to mouth – ? Prisoners tapping – through the walls – words scratched – in the dirt – I – I can't believe – I – I –

LUDMILLA. What?

FRIEDERIKE. The – the Reich – has crumbled – to – to bits – ??

(Quietly **OBERAUFSEHERIN** *and* **GRETCHEN** *cross and disappear.* **FRIEDERIKE** *looks up to where they used to stand:)*

The Guards – they're – they're gone – ? Gone – ??

(No one's on the balcony. Empty. To herself:)

Like they never were – a nightmare – everything – over – finished – ? Was it ever there ?

(She is in shock, frozen, dazed for the moment, trying to grasp what's happened. **LUDMILLA** *stunned too. She looks around, rises, walks around a little)*

LUDMILLA *Am Schluss!* In silence it's ending? *Stille!*

(Another very lengthy silence. **ANGELIKA** *comes to area.)*

ANGELIKA. Such a silence I've never heard in my life …

*(**ANGELIKA** moves off to other area. Silence. Then* **FRIE-DERIKE** *comes to her senses:)*

FRIEDERIKE. *ICH BIN FREI? ICH BIN FREI?* FREE? *Gott?* FREE??

(She then takes off prison apron, scarf, realizes:)

Franziska? I must go to Franziska!

(She runs into shadows as **LUDMILLA** *starts to look around, walk around, then to audience)*

LUDMILLA. Hey? Where's the Nazis? Nobody here ain't never even *heard* about no Nazis? All of a sudden no uniforms? No insignias? Nothing? So. I am seeing Reinholdt the Nazi: "Hey, last week, wasn't you a Nazi? In your uniform *und* boots srtutting around the square?"

(does the goosestep a little, then imitates him:)

Ach! Frau Ludmilla. *Did* I hate it! *Ach!* Was *I* forced!

(smiles at audience:)

Like a baby *mit* its bottle, *ja?*

(Laughs, sits on stool, as **ANGELIKA** *comes running to* **LUDMILLA** *with letter.)*

ANGELIKA. *(ecstatic)* CARL LIVES!

(She crosses self, then reads:)

"Berlin. *Mein Liebling* Angelika – vision lost one eye. Pneumonia with lungs weak. But will recover! Maybe – still – our dream – a clinic in Africa – A family!" Ludmilla – HE LIVES!

LUDMILLA. Thanks *Gott!*

(to audience)

Und me? I am wishing I hear on *mein* Johann! A prisoner of war, *Jetzt!* Georgia, America *Jetzt!*

(ANGELIKA *looks in distance. Then:)*

ANGELIKA. Look! The Americans are coming – marching in –

(silence)

LUDMILLA. But I don't hear them –

(Another silence. They listen.)

ANGELIKA. It's still silent – *stille* –

(Silence. They listen, **LUDMILLA** *runs into shadows, calling back:)*

LUDMILLA. *(calling to* **ANGELIKA***)* I could see them coming! CLOSE!

(She scrutinizes them, amazed:)

They is wearing rubber soles! Boots all laced up! Not like our boys' hob nail goosestep *klomp!*

(She klomps feet as if in boots, then another silence.)

Quiet – like *cats* they is coming –

(ANGELIKA *looks in another direction.)*

ANGELIKA. AND NOW? THEY ARE HERE!

(LUDMILLA *runs in waving letter.)*

LUDMILLA. *Und* one giving me this letter –

(Opens letter scanning it to **ANGELIKA***:)*

Johann *Gesund* in Georgia America! *Und* got a Prisoner

job – working for a farmer *und* picking some kind his "Pecan" nuts off a tree.

(She laughs, glances at letter:)

Georgia got a whole *bunch* nut farms there!

(She laughs more, skimming letter:)

Und the farmer's wife? So nice. Sending *here* pecans! She says, too cold by Germany to grow pecans! *Und* to boots? She gonna give Johann some kind special Georgia *recipe.* Hey! You know what? *Dietrich's* Bakery gonna have THE ONE, THE ONLY SPECIAL 'Georgia America Pecan Pie' in the entire *Germany*!

(She is joyous. Puts letter away. To **ANGELIKA***)*

A big, handsome, red cheeked boy is giving me the letter – even speaking German – *mit* a German name: Rudolph Beck – nice – reminding me of *mein* brother Willi!

(She laughs, joyous. But **FRIEDERIKE** *is looking another way, seeing something in distance)*

FRIEDERIKE. LOOK!

LUDMILLA. What?

FRIEDERIKE. *Other* American soldiers coming over the hill – there –

*(***LUDMILLA** *follows* **ANGELIKA***'s gaze.* **FRIEDERIKE** *begins looking:)*

ANGELIKA. *They* are looking different –

LUDMILLA. Gray – like ghosts…

FRIEDERIKE. They went to the concentration camp this morning –

ANGELIKA. Big, tough Battle Soldiers –

LUDMILLA. Just won the whole entire war –

FRIEDERIKE. But I don't think they can stomach what they just saw –

ANGELIKA. They're looking at us –

*(***ANGELIKA** *and* **FRIEDERIKE** *start backing away to half shadows where they sit.)*

LUDMILLA. Like we was something spooky...some kinda strange things –

(**LUDMILLA** *backs off to her stool, sitting.*)

ANGELIKA. Hear what they're starting to ask?

LUDMILLA. *(calling to area where* **FRAU & AUFSEHERIN** [**GRETCHEN**] *stay)*
Hey! Frau Oberaufseherin? Frau Aufseherin? Hear what they is starting to ask?

(**OBERAUFSEHERIN & GRETCHEN** [**AUFSEHERIN**] *enter from shadows. They each wear a piece of* **FRIE-DERIKE**'s *prison garb.* **OBERAUFSEHERIN** *the scarf,* **AUFSEHERIN** [**GRETCHEN**], *the apron. They come forward into bright lights, each as if standing in separate docks, looking straight ahead.*)

LUDMILLA. *(to audience)* See? They is arrested now – so people gets to ask questions *Ja? Ja!*

(She puts up sign:)

*(***"TRIALS AND ERRORS"***)*

(looks at **OBERAUFSEHERIN**)

Hey! Hey you? Frau Oberaufseherin? They wants to know: does you know *anything* about *anything?*

(She chuckles. In following scene, both **OBERAUF-SEHERIN** *and* **GRETCHEN** *throughout, answer surrealistically, looking ahead, focused on unseen interrogator as if they're in the moment, on trial.* **LUDMILLA** *speaks to them from present, but at times speaks directly to them. Occasionally they sneak looks at each other.*)

OBERAUFSEHERIN. *(smiles, very patronizing:)* How could I not know *anything* about *anything?* I was overseer of Prisoners on several Work Details outside the camp. I lived outside – and was never inside. So. Situations pertaining to assignments of my various Work Details *outside* – I knew *everything* about!

LUDMILLA. *(to audience)* The other one gonna have the same two face answer too, I betcha, I betcha!

(She chuckles. **GRETCHEN** *covertly looks at* **OBERAUF-SEHERIN**.*)*

GRETCHEN. And I –

OBERAUFSEHERIN. *(jumping in, still looks straight ahead)* She worked on The Details I oversaw *und* knew only about the days' work.

GRETCHEN. *(Smiling, confidence. Unctuous, cocky humility)* Because, of course, I lived outside the gates too. But I stayed right along beside the women, marching them from the camp gates to work sites and back to the gates at night where I was relieved.

(beat)

Ach! They were so intelligent! Such educations, class. I would like to say, personally? I felt extremely humble guarding women so superior to me.

LUDMILLA. *(to audience, ironic smile)* Superior women? *"Übermenschen" Sagen Sie?*

GRETCHEN. *(with even greater humility)* Professors, lawyers, doctors, musicians. I felt so respectful…I wanted to make friends. So – when we walked through the woods – alone – I even snuck Red Cross ginger cakes into their pockets!

LUDMILLA. *(to audience)* She is sneaking Red Cross ginger cakes in the poor women's pockets?

(She looks at **GRETCHEN**.*)*

Und this is happening when some poor womens is marching by Village bakeries on their way to work, *ja?*

(She laughs again, winking at audience, shaking her head in disbelief.)

GRETCHEN. *(beaming)* This was happening Christmastime!

LUDMILLA. *(Can't contain her laugh. To* **GRETCHEN***:) Ach!* Christmas yet! *Sehr gut!*

(to audience)

Then they is asking:

*(She looks at **OBERAUFSEHERIN**.)*

LUMILLA. *(cont.)* Did this big shot Oberaufseherin whip the poor womens to pieces with her horse whip? Let the dogs rip them in shreds?

OBERAUFSEHERIN. *(patronizing, smiling, straight ahead, in the moment, in the past)* You insult me? I am a specialist in health services!

LUDMILLA. *(to audience) Aber* – I am hearing she's even signing papers guards have permissions to use the German dogs any time on the poor womens if they don't do any crazy job the guards cooks up! Those dogs? Oberaufseherin's *favorite* choice for punishment! GIs got hold "Infirmary Records"? *Und* worst infection? "Dog Bites"!

OBERAUFSEHERIN. *(smiling, very condescending)* Well…dogs. We Germans, of course, *love* dogs! And many guards' families of course had homes at Ravensbruck outside the gates…and naturally kept pet dogs. And the prisoners? They rotated details. So – some of course did occasionally have house detail: chimney sweeps, sewer repair. Well, we all know how a pet dog can get frightened by a new milkman, a new postman, any stranger, *ja?* And usually will nip when this new stranger comes into the house? But "the most common, worst infection"?

(She chuckles lightly.)

Such a twisting of facts!

*(**LUDMILLA** looks at her silently, turns away.)*

LUDMILLA. *(to audience)* So, the mens keeps on with the questions. *Und* they keeps behaving they is two beautiful innocent white swans floating in a pond between the lily pads. *Ja?*

(She laughs.)

Aber, one day – while questions is happening –

(She rises from her stool, moves into scene begins circling in and out between two women.)

Someone's noticing something Frau Aufseherin's wearing on account it is catching the light *und* flashing. *Und* turns out?

(She stops, close to **GRETCHEN** *looks at audience.)*

It's golden earrings!

*(***OBERAUFSEHERIN***, surprised, looks quickly at earrings, frowning subtly* **GRETCHEN** *has worn them, but* **GRETCHEN** *is cocky. Speaks in the moment, straight front:)*

GRETCHEN. My Grandmother's heirlooms. Given to me when she died.

LUDMILLA. *(to audience) Aber* they is looking at her like they is thinking something don't feel right –

(She begins circling **GRETCHEN**.*)*

So they takes her earrings *und* makes an entire investigation.

(She takes earrings. To audience)

Und you know what? They is finding some list of things taken off prisoners. *Und* a Leah Horowitz survives?

(She sits, examining earrings.)

Her golden dangle earrings is listed! *Und* she is saying her initials is on the inside *und* the date she is engaged with Aaron Katz. *Und* they look –

(She looks.)

Und "A.K. to L.H. May 4, 1936" is *engraved completely* on Frau Aufseherin's earrings! So?

(She turns to **GRETCHEN**.*)*

Your earrings is just exact to Leah Horowitz's! *Ja?*

GRETCHEN. *(very quickly but looking ahead)* My *Grossmutter*'s initials – Liselotte – Liselotte – Horst! And – A.K.? Her sister: Annemarie Kraus. She gave them to her – on the occasion – of – of – her school graduation!

LUDMILLA. *(to her, laughing loudly)* Hey? Your *grossmutter* graduating *school* just nine years ago? *Und* then drops dead on the spot?

GRETCHEN. Her birthday! I meant her birthday!

(She looks at OBERAUFSEHERIN *with subtle, pleading look. But* OBERAUFSEHERIN *looks away.)*

LUDMILLA. *(to* GRETCHEN, *laughing:)* Know what? I am thinking Frau Oberaufseherin's giving these earrings to you. For a present, I betcha, I betcha!

(A silence. During which OBERAUFSEHERIN *begins looking coldly at* GRETCHEN.*)*

OBERAUFSEHERIN. Frau Aufseherin I barely knew.

LUDMILLA. *Ja?*

*(*OBERAUFSEHERIN *draws herself up with disdain, distancing herself from* GRETCHEN, *as far as possible.)*

OBERAUFSEHERIN. There were strict divisions among ranks of officers. She was on a detail I oversaw. This was the extent of any acquaintance. *Und,* as she herself has said: she apparently had *friends* among the prisoners. Sneaking them cakes at Christmas. Also – many prisoners from Block 7 were on our detail. The Gypsy block. So? This likely was Frau Aufseherin's source for the stolen golden earrings. *Nicht?*

(silence)

LUDMILLA. *(to audience)* Hey – you know what? In the final end? Frau Oberaufseherin isn't guilty of nothing!

*(*OBERAUFSEHERIN *removes prison scarf. Speaking in the moment, looking straight front, testifying:)*

OBERAUFSEHERIN. In fact, many Jewish prisoners wanted to testify in my behalf. But World Zionist Organizations in America? Threatened their very lives if they opened their mouths!

LUDMILLA. *(Ironic smile. Then, to her:) Ja?* Excepting everybody *knows* it's your *friends* still hanging around high places that is saving *you!*

OBERAUFSEHERIN. *(still self-righteous, in the moment)* They *testified* for me!

LUDMILLA. *(to audience, winking:)* Truth? Her big shot friends is giving her some kind *forged* legal papers – fancy German writing all over – big gold seals *und* red ribbons hanging down? Says she never *volunteered* for no Ravensbruck – *aber* got *drafted* to go!

(She laughs.)

Und GI Joes is such *Dummkopfs* they swallows it all whole!

*(**OBERAUFSEHERIN** starts away.)*

So? She is going home – but they are telling me she is crying now fifteen days straight.

*(She turns to **OBERAUFSEHERIN**.)*

Hey – you so filled up on your emotions about how you are getting off complete free…that you is crying?

OBERAUFSEHERIN. *(Stopping, turning to **LUDMILLA** Indignant beyond belief, but starting to come apart.)* IDIOT! I – I – cry – because – we – have – *LOST THE WAR!*

*(She bursts out crying now, wipes her eyes with handkerchief, turns, goes into shadows, disappears. **GRETCHEN** puts on **OBERAUFSEHERIN**'s prison scarf. Now in full prison uniform, as:)*

LUDMILLA. *(to audience) Aber?* FRAU AUFSEHERIN goes to jail. "Crimes Against Humanity" they are calling what she did. *Aber* she's sitting there only *two* years out of four…*und* then she's getting out.

*(**GRETCHEN** removes prison attire, comes to **LUDMILLA**, angry.)*

GRETCHEN. Nothing was ever proved! But…because of my criminal record? I can't hold a steady job! I'm cleaning houses and have to live with my old sick father and take care of him…when he dies – I'll take in boarders –

(She puts on gray coat as at start of play. Goes to shadowy spot where she was at start of play, sitting profile again. She sips her drink.)

LUDMILLA. *(to audience)* So – everybody remembered something for *mein* story. But nobody knows exactly that they are "Happily Ever After"? But will as a definite – when I tells them the old guy on top of the mountain? *He fell off!* Died *und* gone forever! *Ja!*

(Chuckles, dusts her hands as if saying: good riddance. Then she puts up sign:)

("THE END AND THE BEGINNING")

So – now the old man's gone, ain't we having fun living happily ever after?

(LUDMILLA, *chuckles then turns toward* **GRETCHEN.** *)*

Gretchen? Gretchen?

GRETCHEN. *(holding liquor bottle)* I told you – I survive – I start drinking mornings – it is vodka that I like –

(She drinks, **LUDMILLA** *looks up to mountain top as* **ANGELIKA** *comes, wearing nurse's apron, African scarf, carrying medical bag.)*

LUDMILLA. Angelika?

ANGELIKA. In Africa I make a little contribution – I don't know if anybody we knew "had fun" or was "living happily ever after," Ludmilla –

(She now touches her cross.)

What I do know is the worst sin we committed was teaching the whole world how far a people can go when they let their greed and fear and hate get pushed front...

(She looks skyward, clutches cross.)

The rest I don't know –

(She walks to shadows. **FRIEDERIKE** *in colorful sweater, as at start, comes forward. Has pad, pencil, phono on. Sits, smoking, she sings:)*

FRIEDERIKE. "Ain't misbehavin, not on the go. I'm home about eight, just me and my radio –"

LUDMILLA. Hey – Friederike? You singing!

FRIEDERIKE. I love that song –

LUDMILLA. So *you* is "happily ever after" since the old man *und* his gang is all gone! You the famous journalist in Berlin, – your husband selling art – your daughter, Franziska playing *mit* the Philharmonic? *You* is *meine* "happily ever after story!"

(She sits, happy, satisfied. She's found someone happy. Then **FRIEDERIKE** *rises, comes to her.)*

FRIEDERIKE. But after the Third Reich? Why *won't* there be a Fourth Reich? Because – except for a fortune teller reading her tea leaves – who knows *what* the future will bring – ?

*(***FRAU LEHRERIN*** *suddenly appears in her suit, carrying schoolbook, pointer. Searchlights start to criss-cross auditorium. She looks at audience – from face to face.)*

FRAU LEHRERIN. *(calling out to audience)* Who knows?

(She starts coming from balcony. She is growing angry.)

WHO KNOWS?

(As if teacher to student, She looks for answer from audience as now she comes very close to audience. Suddenly, threateningly frighteningly, she points with her pointer directly at audience, demanding and determined.)

The answer! *Die Antwort!* THE ANSWER!

(blackout)

End of Play

PROPS

Suggested same be used by all characters, passing from scene to scene, hand to hand. Helps unite their communal experience and subconscious links. Examples include:

–**Baskets** holding all characters' babies, all cakes, Gertrud and her eggs, medical chest for **ANGELIKA**.
–**Bicycle** (if used) by **LUDMILLA**, **FRIEDERIKE**, etc.
–**Radio** used by **FRIEDERIKE**, **LUDMILLA**.
–**Ginger cake** used by **LUDMILLA**, **GRETCHEN**, **ANGELIKA**.
–**School books, record books, clipboards, papers, etc.** used by all characters.
–**Vodka Bottle**: same bottle (period looking) trails **GRETCHEN** through play. First scene to last scene. Scene with **FUHRERIN** to Concentration Camp scene.

LIGHTING

Important element. To create sense of fluidity – moving both in time and place. Some simultaneous scenes.

Also – as stated above, lights alone can nearly create the set. Possible use of scrims for lighting. Bluish/greenish light indicated in script at times indicates we are moving into a surrealistic memory of the past. Once character is in the past regular lighting would come up.

SOUND

Music might be distorted, surrealistic. Suggested that Percussion only be used as SOUND of choice, or German military marching songs, etc. Classical music by German composers used for preshow and intermission.

COSTUMES

Critical to character definition. Especially for **FRAUS**, as described in text. Would be good if **FRAUS** could change clothes onstage throughout – or nearly throughout. Might start in militaristic suit, vest, long skirt, boots, with white blouse as **FRAU LEHRERIN**, The Teacher; puts on white lab coat as **FRAU DIREKTORIN**. Then removing white coat and long skirt to reveal black satin blouse with vest, shorter skirt, leather belt, as Head Nazi Administrator in Berlin, **FRAU FUHRERIN**. Then possibly removing vest to reveal black satin blouse, leather belt with cross strap – a holster for whip, clubs, etc., and several medals for **FRAU OBE-RAUFSEHERIN**. Boots would be worn throughout. Militaristic pins, scarves, medals might be added with each successive character

OTHER CHARACTERS

As suggested in text. Use of aprons and head scarves is suggested as primary costume motif throughout. This enables actors to move back and forth in time with relative ease, by reversing their school uniform aprons and bakery apron to nurse's aprons, maintenance aprons, dressy aprons, Concentration Camp aprons, etc.

And reversing scarves to suit various scenes. **LUDMILLA** wears clogs or country boots, and a brightly patterned long peasant skirt and blouse beneath her bakery and other aprons. **ANGELIKA**, **FRIEDERIKE**, **GRETCHEN** in dark skirts, whitish/gray/tan shirts, possibly with tie, black socks, black shoes as basic costumes over which are aprons. **GRETCHEN**, after school days, as FRAU'S aides, follows in subdued style what **FRAUS** wear.

SIGNS

LUDMILLA should handle all signs as these are chapters of her story. She could hold up signs, announce them, put them on top of each other on a stand as play moves along, or hang them on a hook, one top of other. Also, they possibly could be lowered and raised in some way, appearing as flags or appear as banners.

All Through the Night

Public Domain

Sleep   my child and   peace   at-tend thee   All   through   the   night.

Guar - dian an - gels   God   will send thee   All   through   the   night.

Soft   the drows - y   hours are creep-ing   Hill   and   dale   in   slum - ber sleep-ing

I   my lo - ving   vi - gil keep-ing   All   through   the   night.

Schlaf mein Kind mit Frieden leben
In stiller Nacht.
Wachter Engel Gottes Beschutze Dich,
In stiller Nacht.

Es zittern die morschen Knochen

Public Domain

Es zit-tern die mor-schen Kno - chen der Welt vor dem ro - ten Krieg. Wir

ha - ben den Schrek-ken ge - bro - chen, für uns war's en gro - ßer Sieg. Wir

wer - den wei - ter-mar-schie - ren, wenn al - les in Scher-ben fällt, und

heu - te, da hört uns Deutsch - land und mor - gen die gan - ze Welt.

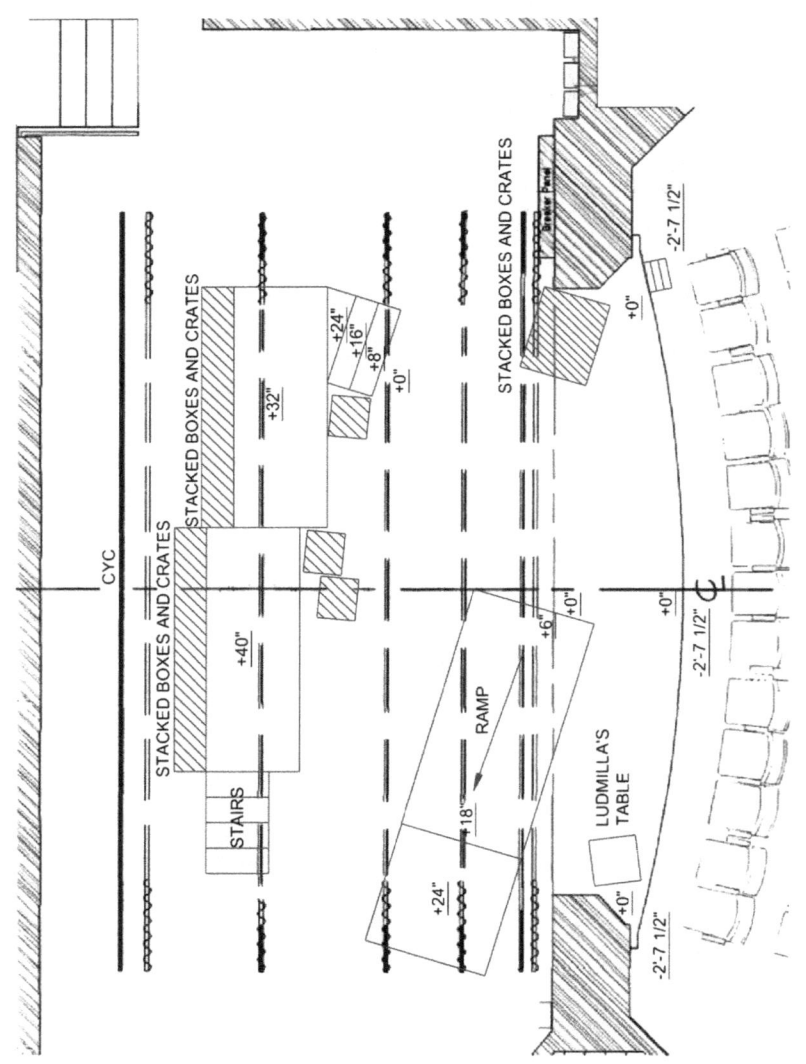

All Through The Night

GROUNDPLAN
RED FERN THEATER COMPANY
MAJORIE S. DEANE LITTLE THEATER
SCENIC DESIGN: ADRIENNE KAPALKO

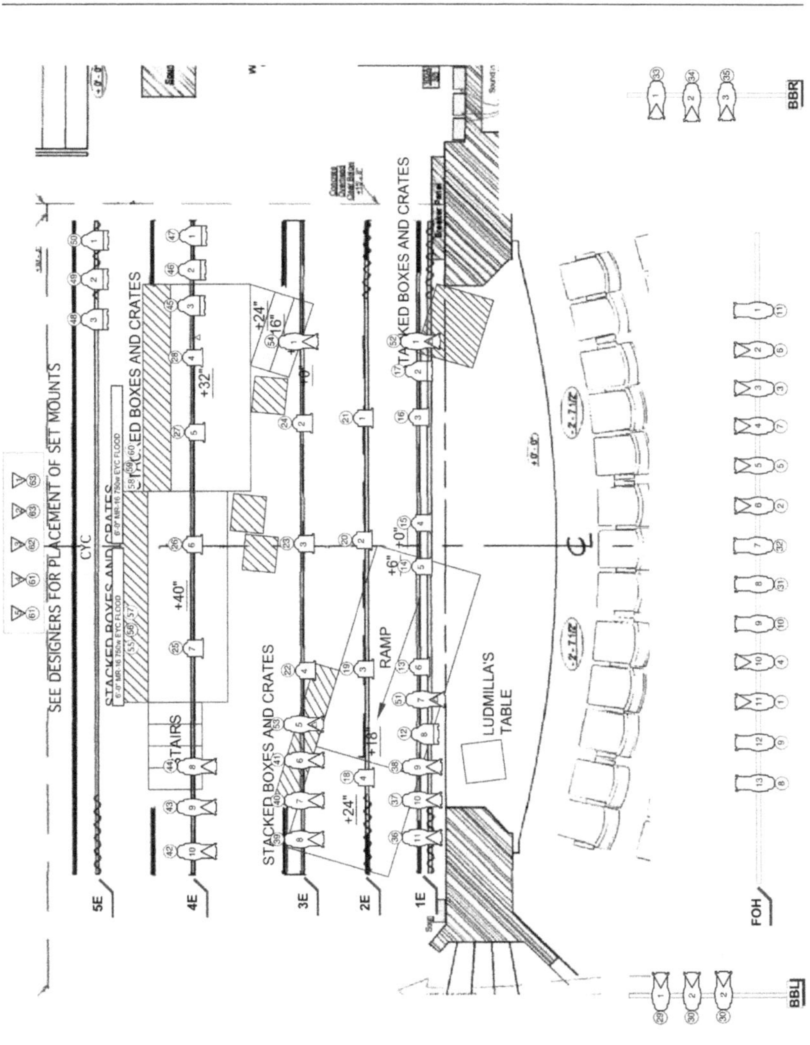

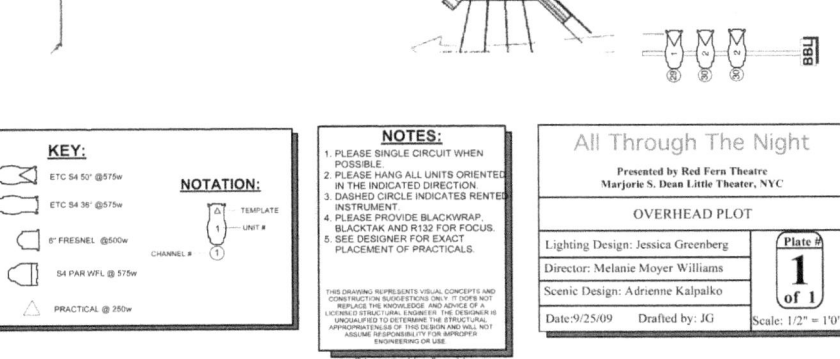

KEY:

ETC S4 50° @575w

ETC S4 36° @575w

6" FRESNEL @500w

S4 PAR WFL @ 575w

PRACTICAL @ 250w

NOTATION:

TEMPLATE

UNIT #

CHANNEL #

NOTES:
1. PLEASE SINGLE CIRCUIT WHEN POSSIBLE.
2. PLEASE HANG ALL UNITS ORIENTED IN THE INDICATED DIRECTION.
3. DASHED CIRCLE INDICATES RENTED INSTRUMENT.
4. PLEASE PROVIDE BLACKWRAP, BLACKTAK AND R132 FOR FOCUS.
5. SEE DESIGNER FOR EXACT PLACEMENT OF PRACTICALS.

THIS DRAWING REPRESENTS VISUAL CONCEPTS AND CONSTRUCTION SUGGESTIONS ONLY. IT DOES NOT REPLACE THE KNOWLEDGE AND ADVICE OF A LICENSED STRUCTURAL ENGINEER. THE DESIGNER IS UNQUALIFIED TO DETERMINE THE STRUCTURAL APPROPRIATENESS OF THIS DESIGN AND WILL NOT ASSUME RESPONSIBILITY FOR IMPROPER ENGINEERING OR USE.

All Through The Night

Presented by Red Fern Theatre
Marjorie S. Dean Little Theater, NYC

OVERHEAD PLOT

Lighting Design: Jessica Greenberg	Plate #
Director: Melanie Moyer Williams	1
Scenic Design: Adrienne Kalpalko	of 1
Date:9/25/09 Drafted by: JG	Scale: 1/2" = 1'0"

ABOUT THE AUTHOR

SHIRLEY LAURO's latest play, *The Radiant*, about Marie Curie, and commissioned by Sloan Science Foundation, received its first Workshop at The Actors Studio, June, 2009, starring Angelica Torn. Another recent play, *All Through the Night*, enjoyed its New York premiere at Off-Broadway's Marjorie Deane Little Theater, October, 2009. In Chicago's World Premiere the play received a Joseph Jefferson Nomination as "Best New Chicago Play of the Year" and subsequently was presented by Ashby Stages, Berkley, CA., and Traveling Jewish Theater of San Francisco. It is a Samuel French 2010 publication.

Clarence Darrow's Last Trial, recipient of an NEA "Access to Excellence" grant, a Carbonell nomination as "Best New Play in Florida, and The New American History Play Prize (finalist), is a Samuel French, 2010 publication as well – while her multi-generational play, *Speckled Birds,* will complete the trio of Ms. Lauro's 2010 Samuel French publications. *Audition* was produced at The Cherry Lane Theater, in the Festival: Turning Points, November, 2009.

Edited by Ms. Lauro with Alexis Greene, the anthology, *"FRONT LINES: Political Plays by American Women"*, enjoyed publication by New Press, June, 2009 and was chosen as an "Honoree of The Coalition of Professional NY Women in Arts and Media".

A Piece of My Heart, whose New York Premiere was at Manhattan Theatre Club, has enjoyed over 1,800 productions around the world, Recipient of the Barbara Deming Prize, The Kittredge Prize, The Susan Blackburn Prize (finalist), the play recently was named by Vietnam Vets of America, Inc.: "The most enduring play in the nation on Vietnam."

The Contest, received The Foundation for Jewish Culture Award, was directed by Jerry Zaks for Philadelphia's Annenberg Center, and originally premiered off-Broadway at The Ensemble Studio Theatre. In honor of its Applause publication, Phyllis Newman starred in the celebratory presentation of the play in New York. Samuel French published the acting edition in 2000.

Open Admissions, on Broadway, received one Tony Nomination, two Drama Desk nominations, a theatre World Award, a Samuel French Award, was a *New York Times* pick for "Ten Best Plays of the Year", and received the prestigious Dramatists Guild's Hull-Warriner Award. Ms. Lauro subsequently adapted the play for a CBS TV Special starring Jane Alexander and Estelle Parsons. In 2008 the play was honored by publication in *Writing Through Literature,* where it joined works by Walt Whitman, Ionesco, Langston Hughes and Toni Cade Bambera in the book's section, *"The Lesson"*.

Other work includes: *The Coal Diamond* (Heidemann Prize, Humana Festival; *"The Best Short Play Anthology"*; *NOTHING IMMEDIATE* (OOBA Festival Winner); *Railing It Uptown* (Playscripts, Inc., *"Take Ten Anthology;"*);

SUNDAY GO TO MEETIN' ("*30 Plays for Three Actors*", Humana Festival); *Pearls on the Moon* (Ensemble Studio Theatre; Stamford Theatre Works with Joanna Merlin, Pauline Flanagan).

Ms. Lauro's novel, *The Edge* (Doubleday [Hardcover]; Dell[Softcover]): U.S.A., Weidenfeld & Nicolson(Hardcover) English Library(Softcover): Britain, was a Literary Guild Choice.)

Major Fellowships: The Guggenheim, 3 NEAs, The New York Foundation for the Arts. Affiliations: a Director of The Dramatists Guild Foundation, Board Member of League of Professional Theatre Women, Council Member of Ensemble Studio Theatre. Other affiliations: PEN, Writer's Guild East, Author's Guild, Playwrights/Directors Unit of The Actors Studio.

Also by
Shirley Lauro...

Clarence Darrow's Last Trial

Speckled Birds

The Contest

I Don't Know Where You're Coming From at All!

Nothing Immediate

Open Admissions

A Piece of My Heart

Please visit our website **samuelfrench.com** for complete descriptions and licensing information.

OTHER TITLES AVAILABLE FROM SAMUEL FRENCH

CLARENCE DARROW'S LAST TRIAL

Shirley Lauro

Historical Drama / 4m, 4f

The story takes place in 1932, the last time Clarence Darrow pleads a major case in a criminal court of law. Set in various places in Chicago and Hawaii, Darrow, along with his wife, Ruby, travels to Honolulu to defend a Pearl Harbor Naval Lieutenant accused of shooting a Hawaiian who allegedly led a gang rape on the Lieutenant's wife.

Winner! 2004 NEA "Access to Excellence Award",
in collaboration with New Theatre, Florida
Finalist! 2001 New American History Play Prize
Nominee! Carbonell 2006 Award, "Best New Play in Florida"

"Shirley Lauro captures…the infamous Massie Case…
a compelling writer."
– *American Theater Magazine*

"The verdict on [Shirley Lauro's] latest play is that it can only add to
her prizewinning ways."
– *The Entertainment News and Views*

"Interesting…with genuine emotion."
– *Miami Sun Sentinel*

OTHER TITLES AVAILABLE FROM SAMUEL FRENCH

A PIECE OF MY HEART

Shirley Lauro

Full Length, Drama / 1m, 6f / Unit set
This is a powerful, true drama of six women who went to Vietnam; five nurses and a country western singer booked by an unscrupulous agent to entertain the troops. The play portrays each young woman before, during, and after her tour in the war torn jungle and ends as each leaves a personal token at The Wall in Washington.

A Piece of My Heart premiered in New York at Manhattan Theatre Club, and now has enjoyed over 1000 productions here and abroad. It has recently been named "The most enduring play on Vietnam in the nation," by The Vietnam Vets Association.

"There have been a number of plays dealing with Viet Nam, but none with the direct, emotional impact of Ms. Lauro's work."
– *The New York Times*

"Brought [the audience] to tears... and a standing ovation."
– *Variety*

"A riveting, rending dramatic experience."
– *Louisville Courier Journal*

OTHER TITLES AVAILABLE FROM SAMUEL FRENCH

SPECKLED BIRDS

Shirley Lauro

Dramatic Comedy / 2m, 3f

A full length, multi-generational play ideal for multi-generational, family audiences about growing up in our "have/have-not" society and discovering what "family" really is. Though teenaged Angie lives in a small, wealthy town, she is poor. Deserted at birth by her mother, her father killed in War, she lives in a trailer with her ailing but loving Grandma. Though a gifted athlete, Angie's afraid to compete at her preppie school because she feels like she's "trailer trash." Just as she is threatened by a disliked aunt who has announced she will soon take Angie away to live with her and put Grandma in a facility, Angie meets a boy at school. Theo is brilliant, wealthy, but an awkward loner. His parents have time only for their country club and try buy him off with "things," while his schoolmates taunt him for his eccentric intelligence. His only friends are his computer and his bird, Speckles. As Angie and Theo form a unique bond as soulmates, they gain the courage to begin their journeys toward adulthood – resolving family problems and taking actions to utilize their talents.

Speckled Birds **was the recepient of a pretigious Theatreworks USA commission.**